THE MURDER OF CAPTAIN JOHN GRAY

THE MURDER OF CAPTAIN JOHN GRAY

By Bill Jackman

A fictitious account of the true disappearance of Captain John Gray whilst serving as the captain of the ss Great Britain 1854-1872

AuthorHouse™ UK Ltd.
1663 Liberty Drive
Bloomington, IN 47403 USA
www.authorhouse.co.uk
Phone: 0800.197.4150

© 2014 Bill Jackman. All rights reserved.

No part of this book may be reproduced, stored in a retrieval system, or transmitted by any means without the written permission of the author.

Published by AuthorHouse 09/27/2014

ISBN: 978-1-4969-9100-3 (sc)
ISBN: 978-1-4969-9099-0 (hc)
ISBN: 978-1-4969-9101-0 (e)

Any people depicted in stock imagery provided by Thinkstock are models, and such images are being used for illustrative purposes only.
Certain stock imagery © Thinkstock.

This book is printed on acid-free paper.

Because of the dynamic nature of the Internet, any web addresses or links contained in this book may have changed since publication and may no longer be valid. The views expressed in this work are solely those of the author and do not necessarily reflect the views of the publisher, and the publisher hereby disclaims any responsibility for them.

First Edition published by Jackman Publications

The right of Bill Jackman to be identified as the author of this work has been asserted in accordance with sections 77 and 78 of the Copyright, Designs and Patents Act 1988.

Conditions of sale:
This book is sold subject to the condition it shall not, by way of trade or otherwise, be lent, sold or hired out or otherwise circulated in any form of binding or cover other than that in which it was published and without a similar condition including this condition being imposed on the subsequent purchaser.

Author's Note

All persons named in this book are fictitious and bear no relation to anyone living or dead, with the exceptions of the following persons:

Captain John Gray
Mary Anne Jamieson (his wife)
Isambard Kingdom Brunel
Mr Peterson (first officer)
John Campbell (head steward)
Mr Chapman (captain after John Gray)
John Prout (Stewart who secured the lounge window)

ACKNOWLEDGEMENTS

Sally Cordwell Director of Marketing, Communications and Development (trustee of ss *Great Britain*)

Liam Tolhurst (Retail and Visitor Service Manager of ss *Great Britain*)

Eleni Papavasileiou (Curator of Library and Archive, ss *Great Britain*)

Peter Revelle (library volunteer who researched and wrote Captain John Gray briefing paper, September 2012)

All the staff of the *Great Britain* who have helped me to write this book

BIBLIOGRAPHY

Captain John Gray (Briefing Paper)
Peter Revelle
Is yours an SS Great Britain family?
Adrian Ball
The SS Great Britain Story
John Christopher
Brunel's ss Great Britain Guidebook
ss *Great Britain* Trust
A Honeymoon Voyage
Mary Crompton (a passenger on the *Great Britain*), 1866

BY THE SAME AUTHOR

Non-fiction
Masonic Memorabilia for Collectors (2002)
Investing in Silver Miniatures (2011)

Fiction
Freemason's Daughter series
The Freemason's Daughter (2009)
The Freemason's Family (2013)

Hurtley Sisters collections of stories for children
The Hurtley Sisters vol. 1 (2011)
The Hurtley Sisters vol. 2 (awaiting publication)

Naked Corpse crime trilogy
The Naked Corpse (2013)
The Elusive Mr Hooper (awaiting publication)
Murder at Gooseheart (in preparation)
Hitching Up (2013): humorous family caravanning stories

Poetry
Poems of an Old Soldier (2012)
Poems of an Old Freemason (2014)
Poems for Little Children (2014)

I dedicate this book
to my wife Jinty

Author's Note

This is to remind you that Captain John Gray was a real person and in truth the manner of his death remains a mystery to this day. This book is fit for family reading and has no sex and little violence.

Preface

This is a crime novel based on the mysterious disappearance of Captain John Gray, who was the captain of the ss *Great Britain* in 1872, and had been for the previous twelve years. Despite being a story of fiction, it is a plausible account of how he might have lost his life, and the revenge for his murder. There is no proof at all that he ever took his ship through the Suez Canal as opposed to his usual route around the Cape of Good Hope, but I have included the canal journey to add more adventures.

Captain Gray was known to beat men with his fists and place them in irons in the bilge of his ship if he found them breaking his rules. Whether he fed them bread and water is unknown, but it is quite likely. Because of this, their desire for revenge is quite understandable.

He was the type of man who would put personal illnesses second to his responsibility of ensuring the safety of his ship and the cleanliness and wellbeing of his passengers and crew. Because these attributes point to such a fine fellow, it is an insult to his high principles to imply that he would have even considered taking his own life without a word to anyone. So many people were dependent on him, including his own family. They were waiting to greet him when he arrived at Liverpool Docks on his return from Australia, just as they did every time he returned from a voyage. He was found writing a letter before he went missing. If he had contemplated suicide, isn't it reasonable that he would have left his letter behind, and not put it in his pocket before going overboard? He was a man of strong principles, and if he had any intention of committing suicide he would have made sure his family had been told and those under his command who would take over the captaincy of the ship also knew of his intention.

If he did jump overboard at 3am, what was he wearing? His night attire, or his uniform? One of the two would have been left behind.

Foul play cannot be ruled out. It is perfectly plausible, as will be seen in the story that follows.

1

Chapter 1

ss *Great Britain*
Voyage no. 35
Departed Liverpool 19 March 1870
Arrived Melbourne 14 May 1870

Gold fascinated Robert Croxley, and had done since he was a small boy. Not that he had any gold; he just liked looking in the jeweller's window. His parents had told him stories about pirates and their gold and he was intrigued when told that men fought and died to own it. He was determined to get some for himself one day.

There was a letter on the mat when he came downstairs. This would be the second letter in twelve months received at his house. Robert tore open the envelope, but as neither he nor his brother James could read, he was unable to understand its contents. He could tell that the letter was from his uncle Sam in Australia, but the only word he could recognise in it was the word *gold*. His uncle Sam had written in his last letter, six months ago, that he was going to buy a gold mine. Robert had been shown the word *gold* by Mrs Smythe, and he hadn't forgotten it.

Robert couldn't wait to learn the contents of the letter, and as nobody in his family could read he decided to take it, once again, to his next-door neighbour, Mrs Smythe. She used to be a teacher. Her front door was partly opened, so he called out to her. 'Mrs Smythe, would you please read my letter for me?'

She came to the door, wiping her flour-covered hands on her pinafore. 'Who's the letter from, Robert?' she asked, taking it from him.

'It's from my uncle Sam in Australia. Please read it for me.'

'It's addressed to your mother, Robert, not you,' she said, glancing through it. Apart from normal family pleasantries the main content of the letter was to tell Robert and his brother James about Sam's gold mine in Australia.

'I know your mother can't read, Robert, but tell her your uncle has invited you out to Australia to work his gold mine for him, and he says any gold you and your brother dig up you can keep. Apparently, he is too old to work the mine himself, and has sufficient money for his needs. What do you think of that, then, young man? A fortune awaits you if you can get out to Australia, but it will cost you a lot of money.'

'Thank you, Mrs Smythe,' said Robert, taking his letter back. 'I will tell my mother the news.' He felt very excited at the prospect of finding gold, but realised there was little chance of his finding the enormous sum of money he and his brother would need to finance the voyage.

Sam Barkley had sent the letter little realising what a devastating impact it would have on his nephews, and how it would affect the lives of many other people. Perhaps he would never have sent it had he known the consequences.

The year was 1869. Australia was beginning to get on its feet, and more and more people were immigrating to find a new life there. Gold had been discovered in Australia fifty years earlier, and new finds of gold had been cropping up ever since, which was a major incentive for people to change their way of life and seek their fortunes in that great new continent.

Robert and James Croxley lived with their mother Agnes in East London. They weren't twins but did look alike. Robert was twenty-eight and his brother James twenty-six.

It had been a struggle for their mother Agnes to bring up two very lively sons on her own. She undertook any type of work and often went out at night while the boys were asleep to keep on earning enough to keep the home running. The boys never went hungry, and she kept them clothed and shod with any clothes she could scrounge, which she kept clean and modified to fit. She bathed her sons once a month in a tin bath she dragged in from the yard. She filled the bath with water she had heated in the copper boiler out in the wash house. When the boys had finished, she bathed herself.

Gradually, as the years passed by the boys grew older, stronger and wiser. They undertook work themselves and added to the meagre income that their mother had managed to accumulate. They worked together to help their mum, in return for all she had done for them.

Agnes's brother Sam had emigrated to Australia twenty years ago. He worked his passage on a small sailing ship which was never intended to circumnavigate the globe, but it did just that. The tough little craft floated like a cork when up against treacherous seas. Sam was employed as a cook. He made it known to the captain that his employment would cease when they reached Australia.

When Sam eventually arrived in Australia he wasn't sure where to start to earn his living. He was nearly out of money, and only had the clothes he stood up in. After working in a couple of hotels as a cook, he soon became despondent. He knew he hadn't come all this way to end up as a cook, and although his meagre wages did include accommodation, he wanted something more constructive.

He decided that the trade he would like to learn was that of a builder. He had never been one before but was willing to learn. He started at the bottom, doing all the menial jobs on site, but learning all the time. After five years he started his own building trade and built himself a two-up two-down stone-built cottage outside the town.

Sam married a Scottish girl who was the daughter of the local butcher. She was medium height and slim-built, with light ginger hair and blue eyes. Her name was Clare. Unfortunately, she developed some strange tummy upset which proved fatal and she died childless, a year before Sam bought shares in a gold mine.

Sam Barkley was getting on in years and was unable to carry out the heavy manual work that gold mining would require. He remembered he had two fine nephews in London who he was sure would be only too willing to prospect his mine and find gold, so he sent them an invitation.

The boys and their mother were Sam's only remaining relatives. He could afford to be generous as he had all he needed. The brothers were very close to their uncle Sam.

Sam had registered his piece of land for gold prospecting at Gawler, South Australia, in 1868. Gawler was not far from his house. He had every intention when he made his claim of working the mine himself, but lumbago had attacked his joints very badly. It was because of this that he decided to send his nephews that very benevolent invitation to come to Australia and dig for gold.

Sam had retired from the building trade and sold the business to a friend of his. There was no shortage of building work in Australia. Sam had enjoyed his job and had employed a gang of ten men to work for him.

He had kept in touch with his family by letter and knew his two nephews were certainly up to the job of digging for gold as they were now grown-up men. The elder boy, Robert, was a fairground boxer in London. He had put many a cocky upstart who thought they could beat him on the canvas for the count of ten. James was learning to be a tailor, but he wasn't interested in the work, and was thinking of packing it in when the letter came.

Both brothers were single and preferred it that way. They weren't short of lady friends, but they didn't want to be tied down to married life. They enjoyed gambling and drinking, and they both took pleasure in looking after their mum. Between them they had reconstructed her house and decorated the interior and exterior.

Their father had left home after only ten years of marriage. He wasn't missed by any of them.

Robert knew he couldn't hide that he and his brother had been invited to Australia, because, even if he kept the letter to himself, Mrs Smythe would soon break the news to his mother that her sons were about to leave home. She couldn't be trusted to keep a secret. Robert decided that he would tell his mother the news; she would have to know some time.

'Mother, we had a letter from Uncle Sam this morning. I'm sorry, but I took the liberty of taking it next door for Mrs Smythe to tell me what it said,' he said, showing it to her.

'Has Doris Smythe told you of what it says?' she asked.

'Yes, Mother.'

'And what news have you? Is your uncle well?'

'Yes, Mother, and he has invited James and me to come to Australia and look for gold in his gold mine. He says he is not able to do it himself because he is too frail and has lumbago.'

'That's ridiculous. How are you going to get out there? It will cost a fortune.'

'I know, Mother, but I would like to go. It would be the opportunity of a lifetime for me and James.'

'Does James know about this?'

'No, he's at work. I haven't told him.'

Agnes was quiet for a while. Robert stood looking out of the window, waiting for her to give her consent, because without her blessing the invitation would go no further.

'It's going to take a lot of money, Robert. Have you given a thought to how you are going to raise that sort of money?'

'I have been thinking of nothing else since I heard the news.'

'And?'

'I have a good idea, but it is only an idea. I need to give it more thought,' he said, leaning over and kissing her on the forehead.

'Well! I give both of you my blessing. I will be all right back here. Don't worry about me, son.'

James was one ace short of a full pack. He was very slow at catching on to ideas.

'James, here is a letter from Uncle Sam. It arrived this morning. Do you want to read it?'

'You know I can't read, Robert. What does it say?' he asked. 'Mother said there was a letter from Sam, and that you had a surprise for me. What's the surprise, Robert? Have we won something?'

'It looks like Uncle Sam has a gold mine near where he lives, and is too old to work it. He has invited us to go out there and work the mine for him. He says that whatever we find we can keep.'

'Is there gold buried in the earth, then, Robert?'

'Of course there is, stupid. Do you think it grows on trees?'

'I don't know; I never thought about it before. Where is Australia? Is it near here?' asked James.

'You really are thick, little brother. No, it's blinking miles away, right over the other side of the world,' said Robert.

'How are we gonna get there, Robert?'

'We will have to go by boat and it will be a long journey.'

'How long? A week?'

'More like eight weeks, but it will be worth it if we find gold out there. We could be millionaires this time next year,' said Robert, slapping James on the back in excitement.

'We haven't any money, Robert. How are we going to pay our fare?'

'No, you're right, that is a problem. We will need some money for our fares.' He had already made up his mind on that matter. He reckoned he would need about £80 to cover their expenses. 'I think I have a brilliant idea, James.'

'Go on,' said James excitedly. His eyes were nearly popping from his head in anticipation of what his clever brother had thought up.

Robert leaned over the seat he sat on and, looking James in the eyes, said, 'We will offer shares to people who want some of our gold.'

'What do you mean?' asked James, very confused.

'Well, we tell all our mates we are going gold hunting in Australia, and how would they like a share in what we find?'

'That sounds a good idea. How much are you going to charge them?'

'I don't know; how about two guineas a share? If we do that we should soon have enough.'

'What if we don't find any gold?'

'Then we tell them they get their money back. They can't lose,' said Robert, looking very excited.

'When shall we start collecting, Robert?'

'Right away, the sooner the better. Come on, let's go down to the Bunch of Grapes. They are open now.'

'We won't be long, Mother; we're just nipping out for a drink,' James called out to his old mum. She was showing the signs of growing old and kept on repeating herself. She also suffered from loss of memory.

The Bunch of Grapes pub was half full. Robert ordered the drinks from the landlord, Rush Benson. Rush had moved over to London from Canada as a child. He was a stocky man who was just short of six foot. He wore a white striped shirt with a charcoal grey pinstripe suit and waistcoat.

'You know, Rush, we're going to Australia gold mining,' said Robert.

'You're lucky; I wish I had some gold,' he said, pulling a pint of stout for each of the boys.

'You can have a share of ours,' said James.

'Can I? How do I do that?'

'We are selling shares at two guineas each, and depending on how much we make the interest in the share will get bigger,' said Robert.

'What if you don't find any? Do I get my money back?'

'Yes, of course you do,' said Robert, getting his temporary bill-of-sale booklet out.

'OK, I'll have two shares. Mind you, I want a receipt.'

'Don't worry, you'll get one,' said Robert, writing out his first ticket to shares in his gold mine. 'I think you will be a lucky man.'

'What makes you say that?' asked Rush.

'Well, you obviously can't see what I have just thought of.'

'No; what's that, Robert?'

'OK, I'll tell you. Your name is Rush, and we're going for gold. Don't you see?'

'Gold rush!' said the barman, with a laugh. 'Yes, you're right, gold rush. That's very good. Let's hope we're both lucky,' he said, with a big smile. 'When are you leaving?'

'Well, we have to sell enough shares first to pay our passage. Then we will need gold to pay for food, accommodation and tools for the mining.'

'Yes, I suppose you're right,' said Rush. 'And you don't know when, or if, you will find gold. You will need to sell a lot of shares just to cover your overheads.'

They were quiet for a moment while Rush considered the practicality of what the boys hoped to achieve. From what Robert had told him it looked a very sound idea.

'I'll help you,' said Rush. 'In fact I am so firmly convinced in this venture I will have another three shares, making a total of five shares.'

Robert grinned as he wrote out the sales slip. 'You won't regret this, Rush.'

'I'd better not; that's all my savings you've got now,' he said sternly.

He made it known to everyone he served that day that shares in the boys' gold mine were up for offer. Soon word got round and there were many investors. By the end of the day, the two young men had sold thirty shares in their gold.

'We could do with another thirty shares, and then I think we'll not only cover our fares, but have some left to furnish the trip,' said Robert.

'That's fine, Robert. It was a good idea selling shares. Have you told Mother what we're doing?'

'Yes, she knows, and she has given us her blessing.'

A month later they had not only booked steerage-class passage on the *Great Britain*, but had bought new clothes and put some money aside to give to their mother so she wouldn't be wanting while they were gone.

'Right, James,' said Robert. 'I sent a telegraph to Uncle to tell him we're coming. Now we have to get tickets to go by train, which will take us up to Liverpool, where the *Great Britain* will be sailing from. We will leave in a week's time for Australia; that's a week today, the nineteenth of March. So we'd better leave home and make our way to Liverpool, so we are there in plenty of time.'

'Sounds a good idea, my brother. Shall we leave in the morning?' asked James.

'Yes, so get a good night's rest. It's going to be a long journey tomorrow,' said Robert.

'We're off in the morning, Mother,' said Robert, as he and his brother carried a trunk full of clothes through to the parlour.

'How long you going for?'

'I don't know when we will be home next. It might be two years; we won't stay away much longer,' said Robert.

'No. We will write to you from Australia,' said James.

'We want to get out there before the rush really starts. It was good of Uncle to contact us.'

Agnes was quiet for a moment. Her skin was wrinkled, her hair was grey and lifeless; it hung down from her head like wispy hay. She had watery blue eyes from which she could hardly see. She thought about what they were going to do; having done so, she spoke to them both. 'All right, my sons. I wish you luck. Have you got enough money?'

'Yes, Mother, and I have a bag full of guineas for you so you won't be wanting while we're away.'

'God bless the pair of you and give you lots of luck in your search for gold. Give my love to your uncle when you see him.'

'We will, Mother. We're going to travel out on a ship called the *Great Britain*. We have paid for our passage to Australia and are leaving for

Liverpool tomorrow. The ship doesn't sail for a week, but we want to get up to Liverpool in plenty of time,' said Robert.

'Oh, that's a fine ship; you will enjoy yourselves on that. You have obviously thought it all out. You have inherited all that from your father. He was like that, always forward-planning.'

'Did Uncle Sam travel on the *Great Britain*?' asked James.

'No. He couldn't afford anything like that. If I remember right, he worked his passage as a ship's cook. The ship you are going on is the pride of England,' she said.

They sat talking, the three of them. Agnes hoped she would live long enough to greet them on their homecoming. James kept yawning.

'Come on, little brother, it's bedtime,' said Robert. They both kissed their mum goodnight, before disappearing upstairs.

Next day they caught the ten o'clock train to Manchester.

'This is exciting, Robert,' said James, as the railway train chugged its way north. The carriages weren't very comfortable and smoke from the train's chimney kept coming into the carriage and getting in your eyes. Then the train kept on stopping to take on water and fuel.

Agnes had made up some packed lunches for her sons. It was only bread and cheese and a bottle of water, but she doubted if they would find much food on the journey otherwise.

It was late in the evening of the day they had set off when they eventually arrived in Manchester. There were hundreds of people massed in the station, all looking for information as to where and when their next train would arrive. The noise was very loud. The boys were fascinated, as they had never been this far from home before.

'Where do we catch a train to Liverpool, I wonder?' said Robert, looking at a blackboard on the station platform. 'Hey, there's not a train to Liverpool till nine in the morning. We will have to find somewhere to sleep.'

'Where, Robert? I would like to be in my bed at home,' said James.

'Oh, grow up, James. Two years in Australia will toughen you up and turn you into a man.'

They both set off to find overnight accommodation. There was a grotty little hotel not far from the station, and the two boys shared a double bed for the night.

Next morning they ate a sparse breakfast of bread and boiled meat washed down with black tea before setting off to catch their train. They boarded the train to Liverpool at 9.30am, and were now both feeling very excited. They couldn't board the ss *Great Britain* until midday in two days' time. They knew that, but arriving with time to spare would help to ensure they weren't late.

By mid-afternoon they were gazing around in amazement at the buildings in Liverpool.

'I didn't know it was this big, Robert. It's just like London. Can we go and look at our ship? I would like to see her,' said James.

'Of course. It's not far from here; we can walk it.'

The two of them set off to find her. After ten minutes Robert halted his brother.

'There she is,' said Robert.

'My, isn't she a fine ship? And so big.'

'Yes, and you know she's made of iron.'

'Don't be daft, Robert. Even I know ships made of iron can't float,' said James.

'Well, this one is made of iron, and it has a propeller.'

'That's marvellous. I can't wait to get aboard.'

'It's not the biggest ship, James; they have built one even bigger. She's called the ss *Great Eastern*. She's massive, and when she was made she had six funnels and six masts, and she has paddle wheels on each side. I think the man who told me about her said she only had four funnels now.'

'Is that made of iron as well?'

'Yes, she is.'

'How do you know so much about this? You can hardly read.'

'I was told all about her by a man in the pub who had just come back from America on her. Apparently, the same man who built the *Great Britain* built the *Great Western* first, then the *Great Britain*, and finally the *Great Eastern*.'

'Wow! He must have been a very busy man,' said James. He found it hard to take it all in. Where knowledge was concerned he respected his brother, who seemed to know something about everything.

'Well, we have two days to wait. Let's go and find a pub with a bed,' said Robert.

They caught a horse-drawn bus which took them to the city centre.

'First we will find somewhere to stay and leave our baggage. Ah, here is a pub with accommodation. Let's go and book in, and then we can look around and see the sights of Liverpool,' said Robert.

'Have you got the tickets safe, Robert?' asked James.

'Of course; don't worry. Relax and enjoy yourself. Once we have booked in we can have a meal and a few beers.'

'Good idea,' said James.

They spent the rest of the day sightseeing and boozing.

'Make sure you take a bottle of whisky with you when you go on board.'

'I don't like whisky, Robert.'

'I do, and I expect you will find that drink is expensive on this ship.'

The time eventually came for them to board. It was a mixed crowd of passengers, though the first class were kept separate from the steerage passengers. There was a lot of cheering and singing from those in steerage as they boarded. It seemed that a lot of their crowd were a little drunk. James headed for the second-class accommodation.

'Here, have you got a ticket for second class?' asked a burly sailor.

'I don't know. I can't read,' said James.

'Let's see it. No, you're in steerage; you go right downstairs.'

The pair set off, following the crowd. There was a queue waiting to find a berth.

'It's dark down here, Robert, and it smells of animals.'

'I know. I expect we will get used to it.'

They shuffled forwards until they found two bunk beds.

'Here you are; this will do us nicely,' said Robert, looking round the very sparse accommodation. 'There's no locker for our clothes, no wardrobe, nothing.'

'It's like being in a rabbit hutch,' said James. 'There's no room to move.'

''Ere, that's my bed,' said a big man with a beard, as he pushed Robert away from the beds.

'No, it's not. I was here first, so move along; there's plenty more,' said Robert.

'Don't you tell me what to do, or I'll belt ya,' said the big man.

Robert was afraid of nobody. His life of boxing had taught him that. He would take on any ruffian who fancied his chances.

'Go on, try it,' said Robert.

The big man swung a punch, but there was so little room that his fist missed its intended target and hit an iron girder. Robert led with a straight left to the man's chin, and he dropped to the deck, out cold.

'That was good, Robert,' said James, staring down at the big man. 'Is he dead?'

'No, just out for the count; he'll recover soon. I expect there will be quite a few fights down here on this voyage. Just you wait and see.'

Up on the bridge of the ss *Great Britain* the captain and his first officer were just preparing their ship to leave Liverpool docks once again for another voyage to Australia. This one would be number thirty-five. She would catch the evening tide that day at 6pm, which gave her one hour before departure.

She had 618 passengers and 170 crew together with a medium-sized farm of animals: one cow (for milk), 150 sheep, thirty-five pigs and over a thousand assorted chickens, geese, ducks and turkeys. There were also two tons of fresh beef carried on board. Added to this was all the straw and feed to keep the animals alive until they were required by the cooks. These animals and birds the captain hoped, like the coal, would last to Australia. They would ensure fresh meat for the passengers.

The coal fires of her boilers were steamed up, ready to turn the twin-bladed propeller (fitted in 1857 as a replacement for a four-bladed one) which would move the huge ship out into the English Channel. Once clear of the harbour the crew would hoist sails and the propeller would be raised up into the hull of the ship until it was next required. The raising of the propeller into its housing was carried out by the mechanism installed for that purpose, and by the crew. This would eliminate the drag caused by the propeller when under sail.

Captain John Gray was born on the eighth of December 1819 at Vaaland in Unst, the most northern of the Shetland Islands. He learnt the skills of seamanship from the age of sixteen when he learnt how to fish for cod with his father on little fishing boats. This was hard and very dangerous work. From 1840 he became a sailor and quickly acquired the skill of handling a ship. He became renowned for his superior ability as a helmsman. He studied and took his exams in navigation and seamanship. Eventually, after having held numerous responsibilities on several ships, including the *Sea King*, he was asked to join the ss *Great Britain* as its second officer. His wife advised against it – after all, it meant a lowering of salary and rank – but he accepted, looking ahead to his future and to where future promotions as an officer aboard the *Great Britain* might lead him. John was a very ambitious man.

He was stocky, six foot tall and weighing around seventeen stone. He was an intelligent and courageous man. He never forgot his own lowly upbringings and was always kind and sympathetic to those who served under him, unless they deserved otherwise.

He joined the *Great Britain* as second officer when it was preparing to go on its first trip to Australia. On the second voyage to Australia, John Gray was promoted to first officer. His foresight paid off, because when Captain Matthews, the captain of the *Great Britain*, resigned in April 1854, John Gray was made captain in his place, and he would remain captain till his disappearance in 1872.

John Gray was looking forward to another trial at sea when he took his magnificent liner on her trip to Melbourne, Australia. Every trip was an adventure and a learning experience. No two trips were the same. His past experience at sea had taught him how to get the best from his crew and his ship.

The ss *Great Britain* was now in constant demand for the journey to Australia, and had proved herself very fast, clean and reliable. Launched on the nineteenth of July 1843 from Bristol Docks and made of iron, she was fitted with the latest inventions. She had a thousand-horsepower steam engine placed in the centre of the ship. This was to assist the schooner-style sailing masts, enabling the ship to keep up speed when the wind dropped. The masts were to enable her to operate independently of the steam engine, and that way economise on the use of coal.

However, the design of the ship now was completely different from what it was when first launched; she had six masts then, but on this voyage to Australia she had three. Each mast was made up of four trees. The wood was shaped and bound together with iron bands. This was all part of the big refit of 1857 and was greatly due to the recommendations of Captain Gray as to how the ship should be modified from the experience he had acquired in sailing her on all her voyages to Australia. Her sails were increased to 33,000 square feet and that, together with her twin-bladed bronze propeller, gave her the extra power she found most economical and efficient. She could accommodate eighty-five in first class, plus 500 other passengers.

Captain Gray thought nothing of climbing each of the masts three times a week when at sea. He did this not only to keep fit, but to show the crew that he too could carry out the tasks he expected them to do. He certainly led by example.

Over the years there had been many alterations and modifications to the *Great Britain*. Once she carried 900 men when being used as a troopship carrying troops to Crimea and later to India. There was stabling to enable the horses of the various cavalry regiments that travelled on her to be housed in harnesses so they wouldn't fall over in rough weather.

The ship was 322ft long and just over 50ft wide and she displaced 3,400 tons, which was light when compared to a ship of the same size made of oak. The modifications to the original ship included extra decks and increased storage space to enable the ship to carry animals for food. The ship required coal for its boilers, so adequate storage space was wanted for that. All of this, together with a modern fitted galley or kitchen, which produced the most delicious food, made the first-class passengers who sailed on her compare her to a magnificent hotel, which in many ways she was. First class also offered comfortable modern accommodation, if a little cramped. This was luxury compared with steerage class. There was nothing to compare with these latest facilities offered to the first-class passengers, providing them with all they could possibly require in a steam-driven sailing ship.

John Gray had married Mary Anne Jamieson from the Shetland Isles on the twenty-fourth of August, 1847. She had eight children fathered by him: two boys and six girls. Five of the children would live to survive him. He and Mary were happily married. She made a habit of meeting him at the docks in Liverpool on his return from every voyage, and he looked forward to his homecomings. He loved the sea, and, apart from his family, most of all he loved his ship.

Although the *Great Britain* was the most modern, she was not the first iron ship, nor was she the first ship to be driven by a screw propeller or the first transatlantic steam ship. She was number two of the trio of passenger liners built by that brilliant Victorian engineer Isambard Kingdom Brunel. The *Great Britain* was the first ship to be built incorporating all four of the latest innovations, these being an iron hull, steam, sail and screw propeller. John had discovered from the start that handling her, and taking her across the world, needed a tremendous amount of maritime sailing knowledge, mixed with a very generous proportion of good fortune.

John referred to her as 'the Greyhound of the Seas', and she seemed to have a mind of her own. She required great respect and kindness. John could guarantee she would respond to careful, knowledgeable sea-craft handling in the most difficult circumstances. He had realised this years ago when handling other sailing ships, and was now able to sail the *Great Britain* knowing that they had a mutual workable understanding, and great respect for each other.

Sometimes she would ride the waves with all the beauty of a dancer. On other occasions she handled like a spoilt child. But John Gray recognised her moods. Instead of bullying her, he consoled her, and within a short while, dependent on the weather, she was back on form and racing towards her destination. He often talked to her and wasn't bothered if he was overheard. He once told a young married woman who was coming from Australia, 'I love every plank of her. I pat her sometimes and I've promised her a rest if she will only get us home in less than seventy days.' A man could get attached that way to a ship quite easily.

John was proud of his ship, and her crew, and they respected him in return. He used methods of handling men and getting the best out of them without bawling or threatening them all the time, though he could shout and bellow with the best of them if he thought it necessary; he could be heard above the sound of the storm. Mind you, John was no softy, and had been known to strike a man if he felt that person was not complying with orders or was risking the safety of the ship, her passengers or her crew.

'We seem to have a rough crowd on board this trip, Captain,' said Mr Peterson, the first officer.

'How do you mean, Mr Peterson?' asked Captain Gray, leaning over the side of the ship to see who was coming aboard.

'Not the first and second class, sir. I was referring to those who are in steerage.'

'Well, we will just have to watch them and make sure they behave themselves,' said Captain Gray.

At 6pm the *Great Britain* cast free from the quayside and the propeller started moving her out towards the open sea. There was a fine breeze blowing, so the captain ordered that the engine be stopped and sails hoisted in its place. One could sense the freedom the *Great Britain* felt as she surged ahead, the waves passing her by at speed.

The voyage was very choppy crossing the Bay of Biscay, and the captain reduced her sails to help those lying in their cabins suffering from the effects of seasickness. Robert and his brother spent days lying on their bunks curled up, feeling very ill, as did many other passengers in steerage. It was sad to see little children and babies lying in their cots trying not to vomit, and hoping things would improve.

When the ship did eventually steer into calmer waters there was a marvellous transformation. That was all that was needed to make the seasick passengers lead a normal life once again. They had their meals and walked the decks to get exercise.

Captain Gray insisted that every person who was able to should get up on deck and enjoy some sunshine. The captain ordered all passengers in steerage to take their blankets up on deck and air them. He showed them how to drape the bedding over the rigging to ensure it was secure and got the maximum fresh air. John often threatened that he would dress the passengers himself if they didn't get up and go up on deck and get some fresh air; that seemed to do the trick.

The women on board travelling steerage were a quarrelsome bunch in general, and were very argumentative. There were many single women travelling alone and many women who were pregnant and gave birth to babies while on board. Many of these babies were stillborn and finished up being pushed through a porthole just the same as other unwanted rubbish. The women mainly gave birth to babies entirely on their own, with no midwife to help them. The screams of the anguished mothers trying to give birth alone in steerage were hell to listen to.

Conditions in steerage were so bad in the heat of the night that many men slept naked, especially the drunken ones, and women slept in the scantiest of nightwear. The food was monotonous and usually cold. There was a lot of moaning, but it was a long while before anyone bothered to make an official complaint to the ship's officer.

The weather stayed fine most of the way down the west coast of Africa. John Gray did not approve of the 'crossing the line' initiation ceremony performed by most passenger ships when crossing the equator, and banned it on the *Great Britain*.

The captain was very strict about hygiene on board his ship. He had experienced the terrible effect of a smallpox outbreak on his ship at the conclusion of his voyage to Melbourne in 1854. There had also been an outbreak of cholera when the *Great Britain* had been docked in Sevastopol during her time as a troop carrier in the Crimean war in 1855.

John was a stickler for discipline, cleanliness and fire precautions. There was no doubt that his vigilance paid off because there had been no reported fires on board. It was all these factors that made the *Great Britain* the most desirable means of transport to and from Australia. In the early hours of the morning, when all aboard were sleeping, John would change into an old canvas suit and inspect everywhere on the ship.

Robert and his brother spent most of their time, when not lying down in their accommodation, in the bar drinking. They drank and drank. They always sat at the same table with a handful of others; there were six of them altogether.

It was a rule on the ship if anyone got drunk, not only would they be barred from having any further drinks, but they would be barred from using the bar altogether. On one particular night the gang of six started drinking early, because they were celebrating one of their party's birthday. The group were getting very noisy and when Robert went up to the bar he was refused any more drink. He was told to leave the bar, as were some of the other members of the party; this included James.

'Why won't you serve us?' demanded Robert, swaying a little despite the ship being on an even keel.

'You have had too much, sir, and your party are noisy. Remember, we have other passengers on board. Also we at the bar have heard swear words coming from your party.'

'Come on, Robert, where's the drinks?' yelled a young man in the party.

'I can't get any drinks; they won't serve me,' he slurred in reply.

'They will serve me,' said James. 'I'm not drunk.' But to no avail. It seemed their party had all been tarred with the same brush.

Robert remembered he had a bottle of whisky in his holdall. 'Come on, everyone. Let's leave the miserable sods to themselves. We'll go downstairs.' They all trooped out together, and sat on adjoining empty bunks.

'Anybody got any booze?' slurred an old fellow, who said he was from Birmingham.

'Hold on,' said Robert, 'I have a bottle of whisky.'

He went and fetched it. Some had glasses to drink out of; others had tin mugs. Soon everyone was indulging and singing. They were creating quite a noise. Drinking one's own liquor was strictly against the rules. When the boson came down and tried to quieten things down, he got a lot of abuse. Robert was well under the weather and could hardly stand. The boson left, and the first and second officers came down with other crew members, to break up the party. The group were all drunk.

'Hand over what's left of the bottle,' said Mr Peterson, the first mate. 'Go and lie in your own bunks, otherwise you will be put in irons.'

Robert swore at the senior officer, and then took a swing and hit him so hard that Peterson collapsed, banging his head on a post.

The second mate drew his sword. 'Right, all of you will be placed in the brig till sober. Boson, get the crew to take these men below and chain them up.'

Mr Peterson was just coming round when the troublemakers had been removed from the scene. He had a cut on his head and his chin was swollen.

The conditions deep down in the bowels of the ship were most foul. There were rats as big as cats running everywhere. It was pitch black and stank to high heaven of excrement, piss and vomit.

'What did you hit him for, Robert? It's your fault we're in this mess,' moaned James.

'Stop talking, keep moving,' said the burly sailor put in charge of the prisoners. The cells were usually empty. The handcuffs were released from the brothers' wrists and they were both pushed inside and locked in. The sailor returned to his duty station, leaving the brothers in darkness.

'What are we going to do, Robert?' asked James.

'I don't know. There's nothing we can do. We will just have to sit and wait till we get released. Just lie on your bunk and get some sleep.'

Two hours later a light was seen approaching their cell.

'Here you are; this is all the grub you get till tomorrow.' He handed them a tray. On it were two medium-sized loaves, and a pitcher of clean water.

'Where do I go for a piss?' asked Robert.

'There is a bucket over there; use that. We empty it in the morning when you get exercise,' said the seaman, slamming their cell door shut. He didn't lock it, but left them in darkness.

'He didn't lock our cell,' said James, excitedly. 'We can escape.'

'Don't be daft. Where could we go? It's pitch black and we don't know our way. No, we will just have to sit it out,' said Robert.

John Gray was livid when he was told what had been going on. Three days later, after careful consideration, he released four of the men, but he kept Robert and James in the brig indefinitely, though he did take them off bread and water after the first week of confinement.

Once every day, come rain or shine, the brothers were taken up on deck chained to two crewmen, who made sure they got some exercise before returning them to their cells. When they were eventually released, the ship was a week's sail to her destination. The men were very subdued and resentful.

'That was no way to treat fare-paying passengers,' said Robert.

'I agree,' said James. 'I would like to get the captain on his own, and teach him a lesson.'

Captain John Gray stood for no nonsense. He knew how important it was to make sure everyone obeyed the rules on his ship, and would take whatever action was needed to ensure those rules were followed; God help those who abused them. Because of his method of dishing out punishments where he thought they were deserved, he did make a few enemies on most of his trips. Some of them were very resentful, while most of them forgot what had happened to them and got on with their lives.

On the day of arrival at Melbourne Harbour the two brothers couldn't wait to get back on terra firma. They had had enough of the sea and the strict discipline on board the *Great Britain*.

'Where do we go from here, Robert?' asked James.

'Have you got all your baggage ready to go ashore?' asked Robert. He gazed once more up and down the quay, searching for his uncle who he hadn't seen for twenty-odd years. 'I am hoping Uncle Sam has come to meet us. I told him when we would be arriving and on what ship. Yes, there he is! That must be him waving to us.' Robert returned the wave in recognition of his uncle.

Ten minutes later they were on the quay. Uncle Sam came to greet them.

'Hello, boys; you made it, then. What sort of trip did you have?'

'Terrible,' said Robert.

'The captain put us in jail,' said James.

'He what?'

'Don't worry, Uncle, we'll tell you all about it later,' said Robert, glaring at his brother for speaking out of turn. He didn't want his uncle to know what had happened on board; no good would come of telling him.

'Hey! Less of the 'Uncle'; we don't talk like that out here, at least not between grown men. Call me Sam, and I will call you Bob and Jim. How do you like that?'

'Sounds good to me, Sam,' said Bob.

Sam slapped him on the back. Sam was tall and stocky, slightly bow-legged. His remaining hair was grey and his eyes pale blue.

'You will find we do and say things different to the poms back home. This is the land of real men.'

Bob and Jim smiled at each other, as they followed Sam to the waiting buggy.

'Climb aboard, lads; we have a fair distance to travel before we get to my smallholding.'

'What's that?' Jim whispered to his brother.

'A small farm, you nugget head,' said Bob.

Sam smiled to himself when he heard the boys talking. They sure had a lot to learn about life in Australia.

'Do you live on your own, Sam?' asked Bob.

'Yes, but I have a couple of Aborigines who work my land and keep the house tidy. You know I lost your aunt last year.'

'Yes, we heard. Your sister sends her regrets and love to you, Sam,' said Bob.

'What's an Aborigine, Sam?' asked Jim.

'They're the people who were living here before the white man came and took over.'

It took four hours to reach Sam's property, which was a hundred miles from the harbour.

'Here we are; this is where I live. You boys can stay here with me or find a place of your own. When you are working the mine I expect you will sleep on site.'

The house was a two-down, two-up style dwelling. Sam had built it himself. Most of the furniture was handmade. There were no refinements like curtains or carpets. There was a fireplace, and a kitchen with a handmade sink, but no running water. Upstairs were a double bed and a single. From the upstairs window one looked out on acres of green grassland with horses, sheep and chickens. An iron windmill-operated water pump was near the house.

'How far away is the mine, Sam?' asked Bob.

'About twenty miles, not far.' Twenty miles to an Australian was just down the road.

'When can we see it?'

'We'll have some tucker, then ride over there.'

They had a meal of cold cuts of kangaroo steaks and hunks of bread, washed down with beer.

'Can you boys ride a horse?' Sam asked, as they finished.

They both shook their heads.

'Then I will teach you in a minute,' said Sam, picking up the empty dishes.

The brothers loved this life already, and were excited about seeing the mine and finding out what they had to do to get the gold.

Sam took them to a meadow nearby, and put them each on a horse. Jim was nervous. Sam got them to slowly walk round the paddock, then he had them cantering. They were both getting confident at horse riding, and Sam was a good teacher.

An hour later, when they had dismounted, Sam wanted some reassurance they were ready to ride to the mine. 'Do you feel ready to go and see the mine this afternoon, by horseback?'

'I think so,' said Bob. 'How about you, Jim? Will you be all right?'

'As long as we don't go too fast,' said Jim.

'No, we will take it steady,' said Sam. 'There is no other practical way of getting there. The road is too rough for the buggy. OK, I will lead and you two follow. Bob, you bring up the rear. Any problems, just holler.'

They set off. The first few miles were plain sailing. Luckily the horses were docile. The boys were enjoying the countryside.

'Hey! What's that funny animal jumping up and down beside us?' yelled Jim.

'That's a kangaroo; you will see plenty of those out here.'

'We ate one for tucker, didn't we, Sam?' said Bob.

Sam smiled to himself at hearing Bob beginning to use the local language. He knew these boys were right for the job of gold mining.

They stopped four times. The boys were saddle-sore. In fact it was too much for the first day on a horse. They would be very stiff tomorrow.

'Why are you wearing a gun, Sam?' asked Jim, while on one of their breaks.

'We have to out here. We have poisonous insects and animals, and a lot of nasty men who would shoot you without thinking twice, especially in the gold fields. There is a death most days.'

'You really mean men get shot that easily?' asked Bob.

'Oh yes, we have a lot of unexplained deaths out here. It's still a very wild country, especially out here in the outback. You be careful and vigilant. Be especially careful near water. The rivers round here are full of crocs.'

'What's a croc?' asked Jim. Sam tried to explain it to him. Jim just couldn't take it all in about this country.

After a long ride they eventually arrived at the mine.

'This is it, boys,' said Sam, pointing to an area of bushland on the side of the hill.

'There's nothing there,' said Bob.

'No, it's not a mine yet. You got to dig the gold out of the hillside.'

'Christ! That sounds like hard work,' said Jim.

'It gets easier as you progress and blast your way into the hillside.'

Just then there was a terrific explosion about fifty yards away. The air was filled with gritty dust. Bob coughed and wiped his eyes.

'What the hell was that?' he exclaimed.

'That's the mine next door blasting out the rock to find gold.'

'Have they found any?' asked Jim.

'Dunno. Let's go and ask them,' said Sam.

The three men cautiously approached the dust-filled mine.

'Hello; have you found any gold?' asked Sam.

'What's it to you, cobber?' replied a thick-set, hairy-chinned worker, covered in dust. He picked up his rifle and cocked it while pointing it at the trio.

'Well, we're neighbours. These two are my nephews; they're going to dig my mine, which is next to yours. My name is Sam, and this is Bob and Jim.'

'Get off my land. We don't trust strangers. We been robbed once, and ain't taking no chances.' He jerked the muzzle of the rifle into the air to indicate they should leave.

'Hell! Are they all like that?' Bob asked Sam.

'No, son, but he's been robbed, so he's not volunteering any news.'

Bob looked around the area. There was a small town of shanty-type houses, a pub and a bank. There was also a general store for all the miners' needs.

The boys noticed some pretty girls walking in the street. 'Where did those girls come from, Sam? What are they doing out here in this desert?' asked Bob.

They were brought in for the nightly entertainment, Sam explained, including singing and cabaret. That pleased the boys.

'We gonna stay here tonight, Sam?' asked Jim.

'I think so. It's too far to return home now, and you boys must be tired. Come on; we will find a room in the pub, I expect.'

They set off to look around the shanty town. There seemed to be no plan to the town layout. It seemed as if the owner of each building had had it erected where he thought it would suit him.

They called at the Lucky Nugget Inn, as the little pub was known.

'Have you got any beds for three?' Sam asked the barman.

'No, but there is a little hotel over the road; it's just opened and the owner asked me to send over any likely customers.'

'Thanks, that sounds good. Come on, lads, we will try there.'

They walked across to the hotel, which looked as if it would fall down in a strong puff of wind. The walls were mainly made of slats of wood, as was the roof.

'Will this building stand up for another twenty-four hours?' asked Sam.

'Yes, I know what you mean, but we are working on it, and it gets better every day. Do you want rooms or a fight?' asked the hotelier, a barrel-shaped lady with massive breasts and lank black hair.

'What have you got?'

'I got a double and a single, that's all.'

'OK, we will take them,' said Sam.

'Let me know when you have another single going free,' said Bob. 'My brother snores so loudly and his feet smell.'

She smiled. 'I will. That's half a crown each a night, paid in advance. Supper is at seven and breakfast is at eight. Any questions?'

'Any chance of a bath?' asked Jim.

'Yes, there is one along the corridor that will cost you nine pence.'

The boys settled up and went up to their rooms to leave their bags. In the double room were a large brass bed, a dressing table and a mirror. There were also two big candlesticks with stubs of candles in, and a picture on the wall of Queen Victoria.

'Nothing special, is it, Jim?'

'No, but it will do us for the night,' said Jim.

'What do you think, Jim? Do you like it here?'

'What do you mean? Just the gold mining?'

'No, I meant Australia in general; it isn't anything like London, is it?' said Bob.

'Stop moaning,' said Jim. 'Let's go over to the bar and have a beer; at least they like their beer cold.' He headed through the door; Bob followed, making sure it was locked.

The afternoon sunlight was still very bright as the brothers entered the bar. There were at least a dozen guys in there, drinking and talking. There were also two pretty girls waiting on tables and trying to avoid getting their bottoms pinched by the randy clientele. Sam ordered the drinks and headed for a table with his nephews.

There was a card game going on in the corner, with a big pile of coins in the middle of the table. Suddenly one of the card players stood up. He had very weathered dark skin, and wore a leather hat.

'You've been cheating, you scum,' said the man in the hat.

'No, I haven't,' said his hatless opponent, pulling all his winnings towards him.

'Yes, you have. I can't stand cheats,' he said, pulling a pistol from his belt.

Suddenly there was a shot and the man's pistol fell to the ground, as blood flowed from where a bullet fired by Sam had evened the fight. Bob and Jim jumped up, startled.

'Why did you shoot him, Sam?'

'Because he was about to kill an unarmed man, that's why.'

'That was a marvellous shot, Sam. Where did you learn to shoot like that?'

'I practise most days. I know I am a good shot.'

The wounded man was clutching his hand to his chest. He was lucky. He could have been killed. The room went quiet for a moment, then broke into uproar as everybody was interested in the shooting.

The man accused of cheating came over to their table. The boys recognised him as the man with the rifle from the gold mine.

'Hell! Thanks a lot. I'm sure he would have shot me,' said the miner, stuffing notes and coins into his pockets from his winnings.

'Were you cheating?' asked Sam.

'Course I wasn't,' he said, with a grin. 'Sorry about this afternoon, chasing you off our mine. We have to be so careful. My name is Bertie Crabtree, and it's my mine you came to. I have two men working for me. You boys new here?'

'Yes,' said Sam. 'They're my nephews, but they are new to Australia and gold mining.'

'You come and see me in the morning and I will advise you and get you started; that's the least I can do for someone who saved my life,' said Bertie.

'Thanks, Bertie; we'll be there,' said Sam.

Chapter 2

Voyage no. 39
Departed Liverpool 27 July 1872
Arrived Melbourne 18 August 1872
Departed Melbourne 22 October 1872
Arrived Liverpool 25 December 1872

The date was the twenty-seventh of July, 1872. Captain John Gray was still the captain of the *Great Britain*, as he had been since 1854, and was looking forward to another trial at sea when he took his magnificent liner on her next voyage to Melbourne. The *Great Britain* was as usual in constant demand for long seagoing voyages as she had secured an excellent reputation for cleanliness and general seagoing efficiency. If she was fully booked, many passengers would delay their journey until the *Great Britain* was available to take them to Australia.

John was hoping to make the return trip so that he would be back in time for Christmas. He planned to take his ship through the newly opened Suez Canal, which would save him two weeks off his journey round the Cape of Good Hope. It would be a more pleasant trip for his passengers, and should ensure less damage to his ship. The shortened journey time would also save the company a great deal of money because less fuel and rations would be required.

He knew he was taking a chance going through the Suez, though many ships had gone before him and had no trouble. He knew from the dimensions of the canal and the size of the *Great Britain* that there wouldn't be a great deal of leeway, and that great care would have to be taken in taking the ship slowly through the canal so there was the absolute minimum of tidal wash.

The captain and his first officer were both on the bridge of the ship, making sure that she would be ready to sail on the evening tide that day.

Some of the passengers had been drinking and were singing or shouting to friends. It was obvious that a lot of them had consumed a large quantity of beer before boarding. If any of them were aware of the strict rules regarding drunkenness they were disregarding them. However, the crew supervising the incoming passengers were within their rights to refuse drunkards permission to board until sober, and many men were turned away.

'Do we have a large number of passengers, sir, on this trip?' asked Peter Robinson, the first officer, who was the captain's second-in-command.

'No, it's about average. The head count is 337, but we are losing a great deal of them en route. I find she responds better with a full cargo. Don't you, Mr Robinson? There are times I think she's showing off. Are we ready to sail in an hour?'

'Yes, but there are still a lot of passengers waiting on the quay. All the food, fuel and water is aboard, sir.'

'And the animals, are they safely housed? I don't want a cow sliding across the deck in a storm,' John said, smiling. Often, when livestock were being carried at sea, an animal would get frightened and break out of its pen and charge around the ship, sometimes with fatal results for passengers and crew, though this had never happened on the *Great Britain*. Most of the livestock were intended to provide fresh food, but occasionally the ship would be commissioned to carry horses or even a bull, and it was animals of this size John was thinking about. On the rare occasions when she did carry horses, they were taken on board in a harness and kept in the harness so that they didn't fall over. This method had been used when bringing regiments of cavalry to and from the Crimea and later to and from India.

'The animals are secure, sir; rest assured I have checked them myself,' said the first mate.

'Good. I'm glad to hear it. How many have we got working their passage to Australia?'

'Twenty-three, sir.'

'That means we have what?'

'In total, sir, we have 132 crew.'

'We haven't had so few as that for years. Make sure they all know their duty and they are watched over to see they do it properly. I don't want non-paying passengers aboard this vessel thinking they are on a free ride without working.'

'No, sir. I understand. Most of the non-payers are gold speculators hoping to make a fortune. Leave it with me.'

John knew he could safely leave it with Robinson. He was a first-class first officer who could be relied upon. He didn't need telling twice.

'Mr Tod Hunter is busy seeing the last of the passengers on board, sir.' Hunter was the second mate.

'Fine. I want him to ensure that all the people who are not coming on this journey, but are on board saying their farewells to those that are, must leave the ship now.'

'Right, Captain, I will tell him that, and assist him in seeing the ship clear of visitors.'

There was a small brass band on the quayside playing a medley of sea shanties. The players looked like little men in red coats and black trousers with round hats on.

John felt pains in his abdomen. He had had the same pains a month before and knew he would have to go and relieve himself. He excused himself from his officers and went to make himself comfortable. The tummy pains eased after this, and he returned to the bridge. He didn't know what was wrong and hoped it wasn't serious. He also suffered from intense head pains, which were similar to a migraine, if not the same. This, together with his fits of depression, meant he rarely had a day when he was not in pain or some discomfort or other. John, having his own rooms as the captain, would often retire to them for a few days, but was always available if he was required for matters which were urgent.

The food animals and their feed were already housed in their allocated bedding areas, but one couldn't escape their noise, or the smell. Some of the non-fare-paying passengers would be allocated to look after them and they would have a full-time job doing it. The quantity of livestock was surprisingly high. There was one milk-giving cow, one bullock, over a hundred sheep, twenty-five pigs, and over a thousand birds: a mixture of chickens, geese and turkeys. Hopefully they would last the passengers and crew till they got to their destination. The noise and smell were quite atrocious, unless you were travelling first-class, and even then you still had to endure the same noises and smells but on a much reduced scale. Only the ship's crew, and God himself, knew what they had to endure when out in the Far East.

Spot on 5pm, John gave instructions to the first mate for the *Great Britain* to leave the quayside in Liverpool. The engines were stoked up and the twin-bladed steam-driven propeller gently moved the ship from the quayside out towards the open sea. There was a good headwind. The captain gave his orders and the boson saw they were complied with. John called to hoist the mainsail on the two main masts. The forward jib sail was also unfurled so that the Greyhound of the Seas, relishing the extra sails, gathered more and more speed. It meant she displaced less sea water and encountered less resistance, so she rode high on the waves. Her hull was not only stronger than one made of wood, but it was also lighter.

Once the ship was under sail, the lifting mechanism to raise the ship's propeller was put into operation. It was a noisy operation as it involved chains and a lifting tackle. Once the propeller had been raised it gave the ship even more speed as the drag induced by the propeller was no longer a problem.

The *Great Britain* sailed into the wind like a graceful swan. The crew were everywhere pulling on ropes to hoist the extra sails. The top deck, or weather deck, was very busy at this stage and the last thing they wanted was passengers strolling around and getting in the way. Everything had its place and the crew knew just how the captain liked the top deck to look; to use an old cliché, it had to be 'shipshape and Bristol fashion'.

The promenade deck was already filled with first-class passengers enjoying the view of the receding shores of England, and trying to find their sea legs because even a gentle swell could induce seasickness. Those who did get sick soon learnt to run to the leeward side and not the windward. Those poor wretches down in the steerage accommodation had no choice but to vomit where they stood. Only time would eventually acclimatise them to the up, down and rolling of the ship as it surged ahead into the breezy winds. Seasickness is one of the most awful conditions that a seagoing person has to face, whether they are crew or passenger status, and it can take a long time before they get used to the sea. They don't want to eat, or drink; they just want to die. It is a most unenviable condition to be in.

There were three grades of passenger on board; well, four, counting those who were working their passage. They bunked in the steerage, down on the lower deck of the ship. It was very cramped, and there was little or no privacy. The area allocated to them consisted of rows of two-tier bunk beds and little else. There was no room to move and in these cramped conditions one had to find stowage for one's personal suitcases, clothes and other belongings. There were some lockers for storage of steerage passengers' bulkier items, but not many. It could get very rowdy, and many fights broke out between men and women who could not get on with one another.

It was an unbelievable hell living in these conditions. There was little air. There were dirty sweaty bodies all around you, no privacy, and families huddled together. The women kicked up a terrific din, shouting out over all manner of things that they found not to their taste. The din continued all the time. They were far noisier than the men in steerage, who generally got drunk and fell asleep. The women were also the main cause of arguments and quarrels between families. Life in steerage was hard to endure.

When the passengers were unable to sleep because of the noise, they either went to the bar or played cards up on deck; the steerage accommodation really was the last place anyone wanted to be in.

There was strict segregation between the lower-deck passengers and the well-off first-class clientele. The steerage passengers had to eat on the same deck they slept on; tables were set around the periphery of the bunks, and only so many were able to dine at any one time. The remainder had to wait till a space became vacant. The food was very plain and uninteresting, plus it was often late and cold. There just weren't the facilities for keeping food hot. The food consisted of porridge, bread, beans, pork and potatoes.

A large proportion of these steerage passengers were out to make a fortune looking for gold in Australia. They had sold up everything to afford their passage, and now they had to make the most of it.

The passengers on the lower deck could get a breath of air on the deck above, but the conditions were very cramped, and there was no crossing permitted over the white dividing lines, marked on the deck floor, to show limits and warn of punishment if one dared to enter an area where they weren't entitled to be.

The forecast was good. John had been told he could expect a good headwind across the Bay of Biscay; this was just what he wanted. The first mate knew his job and hoisted as much sail as the liner would take. The Greyhound surged ahead as if showing off just how fast she could go. John knew that even at this rate of knots it would take at least two, maybe three days to get to Gibraltar. However, he was well satisfied and hoped the ship's good fortune would prevail.

John had another bout of tummy pains which upset his bowel movement. He sought the advice of the ship's doctor, who gave him a medicine which he said should help to ease the situation. He advised John not to drink any alcohol.

Meal times were something to look forward to. In fact most of the passengers divided their hours awake and sleeping depending on meal times. These timings were very strict, and if you arrived late, then you missed your meal and you had to wait till the next one; this applied even to those in first class. The meal times were nine o'clock for breakfast, twelve o'clock for lunch, dinner at 4pm and tea at 7.30. The children were served first, then the first-class passengers. The remainder of the passengers were fed depending on their class.

Dinner that first night in the first-class dining room was a sumptuous assortment of gourmet dishes. Space was always at a premium, but the first class had their own magnificent dining area situated on the lower 'tween deck, or, as it was also known, the poop deck. Second-class passengers used the dining facilities next to the engine. This mammoth steam engine was sited centrally, which divided the ship in two.

In the first-class dining area, the wine waiters were taking orders for the finest wines in the world. No expense seemed too great for the passenger. There were six tables running the length of the poop deck on each side, each covered with a red tablecloth. There were reversible bench seats either side of the table. The back rests on these seats were designed so they could pivot, allowing the passengers to sit facing one way or another as required. This meant the passengers could, after their meal, reverse the backrests and face the centre of the room without having to lug heavy bench seats round the deck.

John had yet to arrive at his table. He was busy somewhere. The captain's table was made up of invited guests. The captain himself usually dined in his own private suite of rooms; this was because he was so busy, and only occasionally made an appearance at meal times. Guest cards were in front of each diner showing where they were seated; there were twelve passengers to a table. The passengers were expected to occupy the same seats each time they came for a meal.

A quartet consisting of string instruments and a piano serenaded the diners as they chatted away. The diners were allocated two stewards per table to wait on them. Watching them trying to balance trays of food and urns of soup was hilarious, especially when there was heavy swell and the ship was pitching side to side as well as up and down. It wasn't unknown for some poor guest to find a meal in his lap or soup poured over his dinner suit, though the poor stewards did their best and accidents were rare. The stewards serving the food lined themselves up along the length of the dining hall. When the bell rang, food would be passed from the kitchen into the hands of the stewards, who would pass it from one to the other rather like firemen passing buckets of water when trying to put a fire out. They stood there swaying with the movement of the ship; it was quite a sight to see.

The menu offered soup, grouse, pigeons, pork and veal. A large selection of puddings (tarts, jellies and blancmange), cheese, biscuits, grapes and the finest port wines helped the digestion until the next meal. Nobody left the table hungry.

Most of the persons sitting at the captain's table were strangers to each other and seemed reluctant to start a conversation with those next to them. Mary and Henry Harper also felt a little apprehensive sitting at the captain's table. It was Henry who took the plunge and started a conversation with a young man on his left.

'Hasn't it been a nice day, Mr Briggs?' he asked, reading his place name card.

'Indeed it has, sir. Let us pray it continues like this,' Mr Briggs said with a smile.

It was as if the breaking of the silence at the table was a signal; everyone began to chat to their neighbours.

'Are you travelling all the way to Australia?' enquired Mr Briggs.

'Yes, I own a sheep farm out there.'

'Do you indeed? Fancy that,' Mr Briggs said. He turned to the lady next to him. 'This gentleman has a sheep farm. What do you think of that?'

'Oh, how wonderful,' she said. 'All those lovely woollen lambs. It must be exciting.'

'Well, I wouldn't say that exactly, but it has its moments,' replied Henry.

It was then that the captain appeared, dressed in a dinner suit and bow tie.

'Hello, everyone; sorry I'm late. Some of the rigging ropes for the sails were tangled and I had to get them sorted, but I'm here now. I expect many of you have already started to get acquainted? That's good. Right, let's have a look at the menu and see what the chef and his cooks have prepared for us tonight.' He quickly browsed through the menu.

'Everybody settled in?' he asked as he looked round the assorted guests invited to his table, most of whom he had never met before.

'There was a huge rat in my room,' said a little old lady, dressed in a black brocade skirt and a shawl.

'I'm sorry about that; we have done everything possible to rid the ship of them, but to no avail.'

'Are there lots of rats on board, Captain?' asked Mary.

'Yes, I'm afraid there are. They breed so fast. They won't hurt you if you don't frighten them; just shoo them away. There is no ship afloat that hasn't got them. We try to starve them out by not leaving scraps of food lying about, but the bounders will eat anything, so we're fighting a losing battle,' said John.

She nodded understandingly, and started a conversation with another old lady next to her.

'I hate rats,' said the tubby woman with a pockmarked face and a big bosom, and most of the guests at the table agreed with her.

The meal was now well under way now, and the wines had loosened the tongues of the quietest and most reserved passengers. This resulted in a very cheerful atmosphere amongst those assembled in the dining area. Singing could be heard from the passengers in steerage.

'They seem happy enough,' said Major Gordon Ramsey of the Light Dragoons.

'Yes. They tend to get a bit carried away, unfortunately. Many of them just booze until they're drunk. They just feel they haven't had a good time unless they are paralytic,' said John. He summoned the head waiter. 'Tell the boson to check the singing from the passengers of the steerage deck. If they are drinking contraband liqueur it is to be confiscated and tipped overboard. Is that clear?'

'Yes, sir,' replied the head waiter.

Major Ramsey looked at John. 'Are they not allowed to drink, Captain?' he asked.

'Yes, they are allowed to drink, but only the liquor sold on this ship. No other liquor is permitted aboard. They know this, but still they persist on smuggling the stuff aboard.'

'Can we stay up as late as we like, Captain?' asked Bert Travers.

'No! Officially everything stops at 10pm. The bar is shut and quietness is expected throughout the ship,' he replied.

When the first course was finished, the ship's captain addressed the diners who sat with him and those at surrounding tables.

'Ladies and gentlemen, I am honoured by your attendance at dinner tonight. There will be many nights like this, and, unfortunately, many nights when most of you won't want to eat; that's how it is for everyone travelling on the sea. In the meantime enjoy yourselves and please feel free to seek my advice and assistance in any matters I can help you with. Enjoy your journey.'

There was a polite handclap from those seated round the table.

'Are you a married man, Captain?' asked a single lady, sitting on John's right-hand side.

'Yes, Miss Briggs, I am married, and we have four girls and a boy. At one time we had eight children, but three of them died,' he replied.

'Oh, how tragic,' said Miss Briggs.

'Yes, Miss Briggs, very tragic. However, my wife has her hands full bringing up the four girls and Robin, my son, especially as I spend most of my time at sea. I can't wait till I return and meet them again at Christmas; we will have a great deal to celebrate. Now, if you will excuse me, I have duties to perform.' He rose from his seat and departed from the dining room.

John never went to bed until he had checked all the crew on duty that night and ensured the ship was properly rigged for whatever conditions might prevail. He still didn't feel 100% but hoped the medication would at least enable him to carry out his duties.

'What a charming man,' said Christine Packer.

'Yes, I was very taken by him. He has those deep brown searching eyes which seem to delve down into one's inner thoughts,' said Miss Briggs.

'I liked his Scottish accent. It wasn't harsh, yet it had a sort of lilt to it,' said Mary.

'I heard from one of the stewards that he can bellow like a bull when he wants to,' said the Reverend Packer. He looked around those assembled. 'Don't forget to come to chapel on the upper deck on Sunday. I am looking for volunteers to form a choir; men and ladies are welcome.' Reverend Packer was a slim man, not very tall. He still had a head full of greying hair, and blue eyes highlighted by a pair of wire-framed spectacles.

They were seated at the dining table for two hours. Then, when one rose to leave, the others quickly followed. It was quite cold on this deck and a draught blew down the length of it.

'What shall we do now?' asked Mary.

Henry looked at her and grinned. She knew what he was thinking, and she loved him for it, but she didn't encourage his cheeky thoughts.

'Shall we have a game of draughts? The children can join us and we can sort of have a winning league,' said Henry.

'Yes, all right. They're in their cabin reading. I will get them and meet you in the first-class lounge.'

'Yes, all right, my dearest, and shall I bring you a shawl? It's quite chilly.'

The children were glad of this interruption to their time. There didn't seem much to do in the evenings. The family played against each other for over an hour. Victoria started yawning, so Mary ended the match and promised they would continue the next day.

Having seen the two children settled down, she and Henry went up onto the top deck. It was cold up there. The only person they saw was the ship's captain. It seemed he was looking everywhere. He had to satisfy himself that everything was tidy and correct before he retired, not that he needed much sleep; three to four hours of uninterrupted sleep was a luxury to him.

The following day was Sunday and the whole family managed to make it to breakfast.

Chapter 3

The unexpected blast on the ship's horn nearly caused Mary Harper to jump out of her whalebone corset with fright. She had been deep in thought, thinking over her past life, and those people she had loved, many of whom she would see no more. She thought of her previous marriage, and the loss of her first husband, who had died in a fire in their farm cottage. Her life in Crimea was still in the forefront of her memories; so much sadness and grief. It seemed that her life was being split into two chapters. Going to Australia with Henry was a new and exciting experience.

The ship had called at Gibraltar many times before, but this was the first time she was going to Australia via the newly opened Suez Canal, which had been constructed three years previously for the passage of ships though the Mediterranean Sea into the Indian Ocean.

The Australian gold rush was the reason there were so many in steerage, and although gold had been discovered fifty years ago there was always a new site opening up. Over a fifth of the passengers were fortune hunters, many unable to pay their fares and working their passage to Australia.

The combination of various classes of passengers was quite remarkable. Space was at a premium, and naturally those who had paid the first-class fare had the largest share of it. Most of the first-class passengers were confined to a cabin with two beds; the cabins were dark, very hot and cramped. There was a washbasin in between the beds. In some cases an attractive brocade-covered settee ran the nine-foot length of the cabin. There was a two-foot gap between that and the beds, which allowed one person at a time to stand and get dressed. The passengers fortunate enough to have a cabin with a view of the sea would at least be able to open their porthole and allow cool air into their cabin. There were a few family cabins which did offer more space for families with children.

Each cabin had a pee pot to cope with emergencies, though there were proper toilets further along the promenade deck. Also there were two tin baths on board, for first-class passengers' use only. Unfortunately the previous users often left them in a filthy condition.

Mary and Henry's children had an adjoining cabin to themselves; they were so excited about their trip to Australia and kept on asking questions. They soon made friends with other children on board, but they both suffered dreadfully from seasickness. There was nothing anyone could do, as there were no medications available. Henry and Mary had already found their sea legs.

As they were first-class passengers they had a private family lounge where they could all relax, and in addition meet other first-class passengers. The second class and steerage didn't have this facility; they had to lie or sit on their bunk beds, or if conditions were favourable they could get fresh air and exercise on the upper decks. Whatever they did, there was rigid segregation between them and first class.

Mary had been on the ss *Great Britain* before. The last time she had travelled on it was when she was returning from the Crimea. There were over 900 on board then, including two regiments of soldiers, or what was left of them after the Crimean war. The ship was being used as a troop carrier in those days, and had very few of the fineries and comforts she had today after her refit. You couldn't move. It was most uncomfortable. Some of the men lay down wherever they could find a space.

Mary had served with distinction as a nurse under Florence Nightingale. She had been relieved of her duties a little early as she had been instructed to take letters from Miss Nightingale to certain members of the House of Commons. They were very important letters, and she had been instructed to deliver each one personally.

There were four in total in her family, including Henry, her new husband. There was Wilfred, who was fourteen, and Victoria, aged twelve, not forgetting herself.

The hot morning sun blazed down on all the passengers on deck. Mary, in a summer dress, was still too warm, and her straw bonnet did little to keep the sun off. She opened her floral parasol, which did at least place her in some shade.

She looked over the side at the crowds gathered on the quayside. They were waving madly at the passengers, some trying to pick out those they knew. A small military band had started playing a medley of marching tunes to celebrate the arrival of the *Great Britain*. The poor bandsmen were feeling the heat in their uniforms of blue and red serge with button-up-to-the-neck jackets. It was, after all, midsummer. Conditions below deck on the ship were just unbearable. The portholes let in only warm air as there was no breeze.

The thought of travelling via the Suez Canal was part of the reason the ship was so full. None of those on board had experienced this adventure before, and even the captain and crew didn't quite know what to expect, though they had all been assured it would be plain sailing. The journey would knock weeks off the time it normally took to reach Australia via the Cape of Good Hope.

Mary returned her thoughts to her life before she had married Henry. Life had been very hectic and not much fun. She had only been married to Henry, her present husband, two months, but she knew that living in Australia would relieve her of the Victorian restrictions she loathed. She had always tried to resist these tedious Victorian values when living in England. Her tomboy nature had enabled her to have lots of fun as she grew up on her parents' farm. She used to ride a horse side-saddle and loved racing across the fields with her friend Henry, the same man who she eventually married.

Mary's memories were interrupted when she felt a pair of hands covering her eyes, and heard Henry's seductive tones offering her a penny for her thoughts. She turned and faced him. He really was the most attractive man she could have married. He was six foot tall, bronzed by the Australian weather, hardly an ounce of excess fat on him. His muscular arms held her gently like a baby as he bent down to kiss her lightly on the lips.

'Don't, Henry. What will people say?' she reprimanded him.

'To hell with those Victorian pomegranates; we're not in England now,' he chuckled.

'And we're not in Australia yet, my dear. I think you ought to show a little tact until we get there, and curtail that sort of language. After all, we don't want to be the butt of everybody's conversation.' she said, trying to be serious.

'Yes, you're right, I'm sorry. It's just that the freedom of speech and the way of life is so casual back home in Australia; it's not toffee-nosed like England. I just yearn to get there again, fast.' He crossed over to the port side of the ship.

Mary was leaning over the side of the ship when someone gave a polite cough behind her. She turned, and looked into the deep brown eyes of another very handsome man.

'Hello. Are you enjoying your journey?' enquired John Gray.

'Oh yes, sir, indeed we are,' replied Mary, wondering who she was talking to.

John could see the bewilderment in Mary's face, so he introduced himself to her. 'My name is John Gray and I am the ship's captain.'

'Oh, of course, I remember now. You sat with us at dinner on our first night on board. Yes, we are enjoying our trip, except that the cabins are very hot and stifling,' said Mary.

'Yes, I appreciate that,' said John. 'However, I plan to put up a sun blind all along the first-class deck, which should make it much cooler for you when we get into the tropics.'

'Thank you, sir, that will be much appreciated,' she said, giving a little curtsy.

John Gray smiled and moved away to greet and question other first-class passengers. Mary thought him a most likeable and capable man. She had great confidence knowing that he was in charge of the *Great Britain* and, come what may, he would make sure they all safely reached Australia.

Due to Henry having lived in Australia for eight years he had long forsaken the Victorian attitudes of England. His whole way of life was so different to that in which his parents had brought him up. He had had to fight to establish himself in his new land. It had been hard. The inhabitants, most of whom had parents who had arrived on prison ships from England years before, considered the country theirs by right, and were hard and unfriendly. They didn't trust you until you had proved yourself. Then there was the continual tension and fighting with the Aborigines, the natural people of their country, who not only objected to the intrusion of white folk, but had to put up with the most degrading and sadistic treatment from them.

Henry had eventually come back to England, having established his own sheep farm in Australia. He had married a local girl two years ago, but she had left him and gone off with a horse trader. He didn't mind much; she was rough and not really his type.

On his return to England, it was difficult to recognise him as the meek, mild young man who had left home eight years earlier to seek his fortune. He was now a rough-cut diamond, and stood out in contrast against the very staid and polite Victorian gentry of his birth. His parents found his attitude unbecoming at times, and had to correct him. He had truly taken on board the ways of the Australian sheep-herders in the years he had lived in the country. In fairness he never let out one of their profanities, though he had come pretty close to it.

'Who was that you were talking to?' he asked Mary.

'That, my dear husband, was the ship's captain. His name is Mr John Gray, and he came and asked me if we were enjoying our trip,' she said, linking her arm through his.

'Yes, of course. I remember him,' said Henry. He grinned at her. 'I could just do with half an hour of you and me alone in our cabin.'

'There is no chance of that, dear husband. You will have to wait till we get settled in Australia.'

'It's this sun that's having that effect on me. I think I'll go and have a beer,' he said, releasing her and heading for the cabin.

'Hurry up, because we will be going ashore soon. Get the children for me, Henry. I left them in the cabin reading books.'

He waved in acknowledgement as he disappeared below decks. Mary felt so happy. It was as if she were having a second chance, a second chapter in life.

Wilfred, her son, was fourteen with dark brown hair and matching-coloured eyes. He was a quiet boy and preferred to spend his time reading rather than joining in the boisterous games of the boys of his age. When told by his mother that she and Henry wanted to marry he had been happy, and the only concession he had asked was that he could call Henry *Father*. If only he knew the truth, and how happy it made Henry, because Wilfred was actually his own flesh and blood. Both Mary and Henry had agreed that no one but themselves would ever know the truth about Wilfred's parentage, and the fact that he had been conceived many years ago by Henry and Mary before either of them had married.

Victoria, who wasn't Henry's child, but was the result of Mary's previous marriage, took after her mother in looks and character. She was twelve, with long, light brown hair which hung down her back. She had a melodious voice and said she would like to be an opera singer when she grew up. She too liked Henry as a stepfather, and found him a fine replacement for her real father, who she had loved dearly.

Henry was a self-made success story. He had gone to Australia penniless, yet within two years had opened a sheep farm and had successfully built it up, overcoming many obstacles on the way, so that it eventually became a profitable business. Mary's family, though very adept at farming, had never been to Australia before, but Mary had handled sheep on her father's estate, so she was thrilled to think she would be back farming again.

Henry came up from the cabin with their two children. They were very excited at the sight of a new country, even though Gibraltar was only a small island.

'Can we see the apes, Mother?' asked Victoria.

'I want to see the Changing of the Guard,' said Wilfred.

'Be patient, children, there will be many exciting and new things to see. Stand close by as we disembark,' said Mary, ushering them before her. The whole family needed to stretch their legs after their time in cramped on-board accommodation.

Their tour of the island had to be shortened once they had seen some of the sights as Victoria had blisters come up on her heels, which meant an early return to the ship.

'How long will it take to get to Australia, Father?' asked Wilfred, as he scanned an atlas of Australia.

'It's usually a two-month trip, but as this ship has a propeller it could reduce that sailing time by two weeks or more. Plus the fact that we are going through the Suez Canal for the first time. Our next stop is Malta and then Suez.'

Henry looked at the proposed route, then went to check the ship's noticeboard. He saw that they had travelled 247 miles the previous day. Every day the distance travelled was put on the board and one could place a wager as to what the distance would be the next day. There was also a list of activities which were planned on board ship. Dominoes, backgammon and whist were all on offer.

John would often challenge men to various games to help to relieve the boredom. In fact John was constantly thinking of ways to relieve boredom on his ship. He still insisted that everyone do exercise daily. Most people promenaded the decks, getting in at least two miles of walking a day. This daily exercise was so important to John that he had everyone from the lower decks sent to the promenade decks to get fresh air. So many passengers were happy just lying on their bunks till the next meal. John would come down the steps into the accommodation area like a yapping dog chasing rabbits. 'Come on up on deck, get some sunshine and sea air. No good will come of you lying on your bunks. Come on, all of you, up on deck!' You could hear him all over the ship.

Later that afternoon the iron ship made her departure from Gibraltar and the family once more settled down to the pleasures of sailing through the Mediterranean and watching the dolphins racing alongside the ship. The sea was very choppy, not what they had expected, and the captain had changed from sail to steam. There were still some sails on the masts, as he would only use steam power when necessary. He had a fear that the coal on board wouldn't last the whole journey, so he was very economical in its use.

For some of the passengers the use of steam and the very large propeller seemed to throw the *Great Britain* out of balance. The massive iron engine, with a huge crankshaft to drive the propeller, shook the iron ship. The noise and smell of the engine affected everyone on board, especially those in steerage. Many just lay on their bunks wishing they were dead. The human body wasn't intended to have to go through such rough and sickly endurance. Many passengers in the first-class department didn't attend dinner that night, but stayed in their rooms, which meant a lot of fine food went to waste.

The following morning Henry found that he was the only person attending the breakfast meal. All the stewards were standing by, but nobody else came to breakfast.

Malta, like Gibraltar, they found wonderful, and this time the whole family were able to spend plenty of time enjoying the island. In fact Victoria was so impressed she wanted them to stay and not go any further.

'Can't we stay here, Mother?' she asked.

'Of course not, dear; we have a new home in Australia. I'm sure you will like it.'

'But Malta is pretty and peaceful,' lamented Victoria.

Mary thought back to her earlier visit to the island when she had been a nurse sent to help in Crimea. The peaceful, quiet harbour they were looking at now had been full of ships and personnel. It had been packed. Not a nice place at all.

Mary found pleasure in showing the family the sights. She had some very pleasant memories of her own of the fantastic week she had spent making love in Malta with her friend and later husband, Major Albert White.

Soon after leaving the island they arrived at Port Said, in Egypt. The family gazed in wonder at the panoramic view of the harbour, and the hustle and bustle of little boats. These little boats, manned by two men in each, scurried around the bigger ships trying to sell them fruit and souvenirs. The sides of the ship were thronged with fascinated viewers all wanting to take in the splendour of Egypt, which had not been available to travellers before then because there had been no Suez Canal and those travelling to Australia had had to go via the Cape of Good Hope. The captain thought it better not to let his passengers ashore at Port Said. He had been warned there could be complications between his passengers and the Egyptian authorities.

It was very warm. On the promenade deck the gentry complete with their top hats and cloaks perambulated with their families; this area was never overcrowded, unlike the exercise area for the lower-ranked passengers. The huge steam engine gave off unbearable heat, though it was only used when there was no wind. Most of the time it was the sails only which gave them their power.

Once they had entered the Suez Canal everybody wanted to be up on deck to admire the view of Egypt on either side of the canal and hopefully to catch some breeze. The sun blazed down. It was so bad that the captain had the top deck covered along its length with a long parasol supported and strung together so that all on the deck were protected against the sun; even the poultry and the cow reserved for milking enjoyed this luxury.

'Look, Father, there's the pyramids,' shouted Wilfred gleefully, as the long iron ship made history, being the first of her kind to sail along the canal. The ship's speed was very slow, as the width of the canal was nearly the same as the width of the ship herself. The captain knew he mustn't make any waves.

The children, like many other people, were dashing from side to side to take in as many views as possible. An Arab, walking along the canal side leading an ungainly camel, waved at the passengers, who politely responded. Some shouted out greetings. It was the first time most of them had seen anything of Egypt.

It was such a wonderful feeling sailing through the Suez Canal. Very few boats the size of the *Great Britain* had passed through since it had been opened in November, three years earlier, but numbers were increasing.

'Where does the Suez Canal finish, Father?' asked Wilfred, who was the most inquisitive member of the family.

'It joins up with the Red Sea, my son,' his father replied, as he tried to shield his eyes from the glare of the fierce midday sun.

'Look, Father, we are coming into a lake,' said Victoria, bewildered.

'Yes, my dear; it is called "the Bitter Lake" and has been built so that ships can pass each other, which they can't do on the canal. Each ship will have to wait its turn to proceed further, and take it only when the canal is clear.'

'It's all very exciting, Father,' said Wilfred, who was taking it all in.

'Tell me some more details about the sheep farm, darling,' Mary said.

'I've told you lots before when we were in England,' replied Henry.

'I know, but it's different now. I am actually going to be part of it. Did I tell you I dreamt about your sheep farm more than once when I was a nurse in Crimea?'

'All right; let's sit here, where there is a little shade. I appreciate it is all strange to you, my love, but I know you will be happy there, and I can think of no lovelier girl than you to share it with.'

Mary kissed him on the cheek in recognition of his kind words.

'I'm going off with my friend Jennifer for a walk around the ship,' said Victoria. 'Come on, Wilfred, come and join us.'

'No, thank you,' said Wilfred. 'Mother, I'm bored. Father, did you bring any books with you?'

'I have some books on sheep farming,' answered Henry. 'I don't know if they will be of any interest to you. However, you are welcome to read them. I could do with all the help I can get when we get to Australia. I hope you will help me in the running of the place. Do you want the books?'

'Yes please, Father. I am interested, although I have already studied the climate and conditions out there a great deal.'

'Well, you may fetch them. They are under my bed in our cabin. There are three of them.'

'It's nice to know he's interested, my love,' Mary said, watching Wilfred's departure. 'I know he will grow up to be a son you can love and respect.'

'I do already,' he said, giving her a gentle squeeze round the waist.

'What will I be doing, Henry? Can I work with the sheep? Remember, I worked on my father's estate and helped at lambing time.'

'Of course you can. That's why I married you, so I could have an extra unpaid hand on the farm.' He grinned.

'Who does the cooking and house cleaning?'

'Not you. We have some Aborigines who do all that. Murky is the cook, and Scrumpy is the housemaid. She's a little darling; you will like her.'

'Have we got neighbours?'

'Why, of course. The Kingston family aren't far away.'

'How far?'

'Only about a hundred miles or so.'

Mary looked at him in disbelief. 'You are joking, aren't you?' she asked, hoping that he was.

'No, I'm sorry to say I'm not. Australia is a massive country compared with England, and sparsely populated. The more shiploads of people who go there, the quicker it will grow, and there will be nearer neighbours.'

Mary didn't like the idea of such isolation, but kept her own counsel; all would be revealed in time.

'No, I was joking. There is a little shanty town with a general store, a pub and a bank, and a few houses. It's growing all the time. It seems to have all sprung up in the last five years; before that there was nothing.'

Suddenly the quietness was shattered by the sound of the ship's alarm system. The hooter gave three loud blasts. What could be wrong? The ship's bow swung sharply to the port side, there was a loud crunching noise and the ship came abruptly to a halt. Standing passengers who were not holding on to a rail were flung forward. Henry and Mary felt themselves lifted from their seats by the force of the impact.

'What's the matter?' cried Mary. 'Are we sinking? What was that bump, Henry?' She wasn't alone in her concern; all the other passengers looked worried and scared.

'We have hit something. I don't know what. Wait here.' Henry went to the rail to see what had caused the sudden stop. As he could see nothing, he crossed to the other side. The ship was at angles across the Suez, its nose stuck in the river bank. Several elderly people had been slightly hurt in the collision. Mary, ignoring Henry's instruction to stay put, went to see if she could be of help.

There was a good deal of screaming from passengers alarmed at this unscheduled stop. The ship's crew were running everywhere, trying to pacify passengers and answer questions from irate travellers demanding to know the reason for the collision they had concluded there must have been.

Henry grabbed the arm of a passing sailor. 'What has happened?' he demanded.

'It appears we have run into the bank, sir. A small fishing boat cut right in front of us. We had a choice: either run it down or take evasive action. That's why the captain blew the ship's hooter.'

Thanking him, Henry looked over the side to where the bow of the ship had embedded itself firmly into the canal bank. The captain was trying to release his vessel by continually putting it into reverse gear, but in vain.

'Ladies and gentlemen,' the captain announced through a loud-hailer. 'Don't be alarmed. We have run into the bank and are jammed. The reason is that we tried to avoid an accident with a fishing boat. I don't think there is any serious damage and assistance is on its way. Please don't worry. I will keep you informed.'

Gradually, normality resumed and interest in the accident subsided as passengers continued their various relaxations.

Victoria came running up to Mary. 'Mother, Father, are you all right? Isn't it exciting? Where's Wilfred?'

'I don't know. In the cabin, I assume. You had better check on him, Henry. He may have been injured.'

Henry and Victoria went to find Wilfred. Opening the cabin door, they saw Wilfred lying on the floor. A big wardrobe had become detached in the collision and had come crashing down on him, pinning him beneath it.

'Wilfred! Wilfred!' Henry called. There was no reply. 'Victoria, go and tell Mother what has happened. Tell her we need a doctor here quickly.'

While Victoria rushed off to find her mother, Henry lifted the wardrobe back to its position. The boy stirred and moaned.

'Hold on, son. Help is on the way. Where does it hurt?'

'It's my leg and ankle, Father, that's where the pain is,' Wilfred said, trying to nurse his injury, but it was too tender to touch.

It was twenty minutes before the ship's doctor arrived. A chubby fellow with grey hair and watery blue eyes, he seemed very old. Wearing a tweed suit and waistcoat and hat, with a gold watch and chain, he looked completely overdressed for the tropics.

'I'm sorry I'm late,' he said, looking around the cabin, 'but the collision has given us a great many casualties. Is this your son?'

'Yes. He's in great pain. That big wardrobe has fallen on him and damaged his leg,' said Henry.

'Yes, I see.' The doctor opened his medical bag and took out a stethoscope. Upon examining the boy he pronounced that it was a broken leg.

'Don't worry, young man, we will soon have you in splints,' said the doctor, smiling at him. He turned to Henry. 'Wait here with your son and I will have some deckhands bring him to the medical bay.'

Ten minutes later two crew members came and took Wilfred to the sick bay, with Mary at his side, reassuring him that he would be all right.

Later that afternoon a tug ship appeared from Aden. The passengers were told not to go to one side all together, as it would make the freeing of the ship more difficult and could even result in the ship capsizing.

Wilfred was to spend the night in the ship's hospital and was to rejoin the family the next day. He seemed happy enough, surrounded by books.

It was while they were having their evening meal that the captain made his announcement.

'Ladies and gentlemen, I am sorry to tell you that we will have to evacuate the ship. We cannot refloat it while there are so many people on board, so at eight o'clock I want everyone to disembark. The crew will be there to help you. Take with you blankets and whatever you need for the night.'

At eight o'clock the boat stations were manned and an organised disembarkation proceeded. One old lady fell into the canal trying to save her dog; there were no further incidents. The night was dry but very cold and they needed their blankets.

Just before dawn, a patrol of Egyptian police went on board and spoke to the captain. It appeared that all the ship's crew and passengers standing on Egyptian soil were under arrest for landing illegally without the proper paperwork.

'That's bloody absurd,' said John, to the chief of police.

'I am sorry, Captain, you have broken the law. I am at liberty to impound your ship and take you all away to a prison to await trial,' said the police chief.

John shook his head in disbelief.

The chief of police gave instructions to his second-in-command. 'Have transport sent for; we will need many wagons to take all these passengers to Cairo.'

In the meantime, the tug and the workmen kept on working and eventually freed the boat. The captain tried to get his passengers back.

'Wait! Is there no other way this can be resolved? We have the ship free from the canal bank and are ready to sail. We can be away in an hour at the latest,' said John. He removed his cap and scratched his head of receding hair, trying to find a solution which would save face for both parties.

'This is most unusual, Captain. However, rather than put these poor people through another cold and uncomfortable night, I will accept 500 English sovereigns for their release.'

John was livid when he heard the alternative to prison in Egypt. This was clearly illegal, but with so much at risk he was not inclined to argue.

'If I pay you this money, will you guarantee I will have no more trouble from your authorities?'

The policeman smiled at him. 'I assure you, sir, you may safely proceed on your way.'

John instructed his purser to arrange the payment. True to his word, once he had been paid, the policeman disappeared with his men into what remained of the night. The ship was checked for structural damage but nothing of any importance was found that would delay their departure, and so the journey continued.

Their next stop was Aden, where the ship took on water and coal. John reckoned he had enough coal, but he took on board another twenty tons, just in case; besides, it was a better price than back home. John, being a Scotsman, wasn't mean, but he was very careful.

No one went ashore at Aden as there was nothing of any consequence to see. However, the ship was given a thorough inspection to ensure her safe passage to Australia. The bow was a little dented, but the soft sandy bank had cushioned most of the impact.

Chapter 4

They were two weeks out from Liverpool. By now most of the passengers had found their sea legs and were able to cope with the ship's ducking and diving. There had been a few fights amongst the passengers in steerage, nothing serious. Many tempers were on a short fuse, especially after they had been on the beer.

Tod Hunter, the second mate, was carrying out his daily round of inspection of each deck to see that everything was satisfactory. He told Mr Simpson, the subaltern accompanying him, to take notes of anything that displeased Hunter and needed attention.

As they neared the steerage-class accommodation they were approached by two men. They were what Tod would refer to as labourers. Dressed in trousers with braces, long-sleeved shirts and shoes. These two men blocked the way of the inspecting officers.

'May we pass, please?' asked Tod.

'No, you bloody can't. Not till you've sorted out our problem,' said the taller, stockier man of the two.

'That's what we're here for: to find out if everyone is happy and contented,' said Mr Hunter. 'What is the nature of your complaint, gentlemen?'

'We're fed up with cold meals and boring stale food that always arrives too late. That's not just from us two but from every one of the passengers in steerage.'

'I'm sorry to hear that. It shouldn't be that way. Write down the complaint, Simpson, and we will get it sorted out,' said Mr Hunter.

'Can I have your names, please?' Mr Simpson asked the men.

'What for?'

'We like to know who we are talking to, and it will assist us when we get the matter sorted, or we have to get back to you.'

'All right, my name is Jake Spears, and this 'ere is Toby Dowdy.'

The ship's officers proceeded on their inspection with no further complaints.

The steerage accommodation stank of beer, piss and vomit mainly, but there were many other odours mixed in with them. Many people were lying asleep, some chatting, but the sound of crying babies and children seemed to predominate over everything else. There seemed to be a new baby born every week. Its poor mother had to rely on the help of other women on board in giving birth. Most of the babies died at birth; some lived for a few months. Most of the women looked washed out. They had drawn faces with eyes that looked at you as if saying, 'Please help us, life is hell in steerage.'

You couldn't move along the gangway between the bunks; packing cases were everywhere. Many of the passengers slept sitting up, using the rest of the space to stow their baggage. Close by was where the sheep and poultry were being kept, and although they were cleaned out daily there was no escaping the smell and the noise from them.

Mr Hunter reported the incident to John. He had expected this and had experienced similar complaints on most of his trips to Australia and back. There was nothing that could be done. It was all down to numbers and space limitations, the distance food had to travel and of course the priority of class.

Two weeks later a gang of four men came into the galley, and they included Jake Spears and Toby Dowdy. They started complaining to the catering staff about cold, boring food and how they wanted it to improve. The master cook tried to help by explaining his staff's duties and the food allocation. They weren't satisfied and tried to get to see the captain. Their path was blocked by the stewards and the captain was sent for.

'Right! What's all this fuss about?' demanded John.

'We're here to complain about the food, and conditions. We are steerage passengers and don't want to live in a pigsty; it's disgusting,' said a little Cornishman.

'There is nothing that can be done about the food,' said John.

'We want better food. Ours is cold, and boring. Why can't we have the same as first class?'

'Because you haven't paid anywhere near the money that they have paid for their food.'

'Why is our food cold when we get it?'

'There are three reasons why we can't keep the food hot. One is that we have no ways of doing this. Second is the space limitation, and third the distance needed to take the food from the galley to where you are feeding. We do our best,' said John. 'Now return to your families.'

'You're not getting away with those simple reasons. You're the captain; perhaps you need to be taught a lesson. Take that,' said Toby Dowdy, who was a big man with one eye. He swung a punch at the captain. John took it on the chin, but the blow knocked him down.

Mr Peterson, the first officer, drew his sword. 'Put these four men in the brig,' he told the stewards who had accumulated to hear the row. 'Feed them bread and water for one week.'

The four men struggled, but were held secure by the deckhands and stewards.

Mr Peterson helped John to his feet. 'Are you all right, sir?'

'Yes; he caught me unawares. He won't catch me again,' said John, rubbing his chin.

The Mediterranean Sea was unpredictable. One day it was fine and sunny; the next, rough seas and squalls. The sea was sometimes so bad one thought that the *Great Britain* would be broken into pieces. However, the ship showed her prowess. She pushed her bow forward into the gales. John often thought she was enjoying it.

The days could be long and boring in bad weather. Most passengers lay on their bunks sleeping. Everyone was looking forward to the next meal, if they could make it.

After the disturbance with the Cornish men there was a lot of bad feeling from those in steerage. John was wary that the situation could deteriorate even further, so he asked for a representational party of steerage passengers to meet him in the dining area and try to sort the complaints out. They wanted the four men who were detained in the brig to be released. John agreed to let three out but keep one in chains. They begrudgingly accepted this. He also sorted out other disagreements, and eventually the air was clearer and the committee returned to their quarters.

Three of the men held in the brig were released, but Toby Dowdy, the man who had knocked the captain down, was not; he would stay there indefinitely. The conditions in the bowels of the ship where the prisoners were housed were very unpleasant; they were damp, dark and noisy. Most of the smaller animals were stored in the same area, so the bad boys didn't get much sleep and the stench was awful.

There had been a similar incident four years earlier, when a fight between steerage passengers had concluded when one had taken a knife and stabbed the other. The assailant had been kept in prison for the journey and handed over to the Australian police, who had put him in prison.

Most of the trouble in steerage was caused through alcohol. There were very strict rules on board to try to keep alcohol consumption to a minimum.

The church service in the improvised chapel on the poop deck was laid out to accommodate the first-class passengers only. The parson, Reverend Packer, had managed to form a choir, though most of the volunteers had been pressed to join. The sermon passed a pleasant hour, and the ship sailed in calm water during this period. This was followed by Holy Communion for those wishing to take part. It gave a sort of normality to what could be a dreary Sunday at sea.

Life aboard the *Great Britain* had by now fallen into regularity. One knew what was programmed for entertainment, and the menus were changed daily. Mary found that the first-class passenger lounge offered comforts on board she could not find anywhere else. It gave her and the children the opportunity to read, play-act, play games and mix with the other first-class passengers, most of whom were very nice people and easy to get along with.

They stopped at Colombo and saw cows walking in the high street, which Victoria thought very strange. Wilfred was not able to join the family ashore and had to content himself with the view from his cabin window. There was so much for the young family to see and learn about. Henry and Mary were blissfully happy. Henry was in his element in his new role of father, and relished broadening his family's education in all aspects of life and travel.

Mary stood close to Henry, looking over the side of the liner as she slowly made her way through to the Indian Ocean. It was a quiet evening, with just the *thud, thud* of the engine as the crew nursed the liner through the calm waters. It was so pleasant and cool after the sweltering heat of the day. Apparently, sleeping on deck was permitted in such weather.

Wilfred's leg was mending and he was now hobbling about. It would only be a matter of days before he was well enough to have the splint removed.

Suddenly Mary felt a change in temperature. She pulled her shawl closer round her shoulders.

'My! It's suddenly got a lot colder and, look, there are dark clouds scudding across the sky. Do you think we are in for a storm?'

'Quite likely,' said Henry, putting his arm round her waist. 'They can be sudden and very fierce out here. Come on; let's go down to our cabin.'

It being the monsoon period, sudden storms were to be expected. It was at night that the squall hit the boat. First there were high winds. They were so fierce that the captain had to reduce sail drastically and just stay on the engine. It was in stormy conditions such as these that the value of having both sail and steam was confirmed.

The vessel swayed from left to right and up and down at the same time. These gyrations caused most of the passengers to become seasick.

Water came down the hatchways and flooded the corridors. Everything that wasn't fastened down fell on the floor.

The storm raged on. It was like riding a bucking bronco, thought Henry. Suddenly there was an almighty crash that could be heard throughout the ship.

'Mother, what was that bang? I'm frightened,' squealed Victoria. Wilfred put his arm round his sister to comfort her.

'I think that was a mast which has broken,' Henry said. 'It happened the first time I went to Australia.'

'Oh dear, this ship does seem unlucky, Henry. Do you think we will make it to Australia?' Mary could hear passengers running up and down the corridors, many of them terrified.

'Of course we will, my dear. You experienced worse storms than this when you sailed to Crimea, or have you forgotten?'

'I know, Henry. We had to throw the guns overboard to stop the ship sinking, but I didn't have to worry about my family in those days,' she reminded him.

'Have you been to sea in worse storms than this, then, Mother?' asked Wilfred.

'Yes, dear, a lot worse. I'll tell you all about it one day.'

The storm seemed to be getting worse. The ship was banging down hard on the waves, making the whole vessel shudder.

'I feel so ill. How long is this going to last?' sobbed Victoria.

'I don't know, Victoria. Be a brave little girl. It's what is known as seasickness. I know it's unpleasant, but it will pass. I have it as well, but we must be brave,' said Mary, cuddling her daughter. 'There is no cure for it, I'm afraid, my dear.'

'What shall we do? Are we going to sink?' Victoria looked as white as the sea boiling around the ship.

'Don't worry, my darling. You will be safe. This ship was made to fight its way through the biggest storms,' said Mary, looking at Henry for confirmation.

Wilfred lay on his bunk facing the wall and saying nothing. The wind was still howling and the boat wallowed in the heavy seas, making little progress. Mary reached out her hand and grasped Henry's. She wanted reassurance and also wanted to show him she wasn't afraid as long as she had him with her. He leaned over and kissed her.

'Come on, family, there is nothing we can do. Let's go to bed and try to get some sleep. Remember, God is watching over us,' said Mary, tucking her children into their bunks.

No one slept much, and the storm continued throughout the night. At dawn, a dreary light filtered through the water-covered portholes. There was nothing to be seen but the high seas. One moment the ship was in a hollow; the next it was on a high crest, when the passengers could look out across the tormented waters, hoping to see land. At last the wind had dropped and the sun was beginning to shine again.

'Anyone for breakfast?' asked Henry, with a grin. 'I'm going. Who's coming with me?'

'Not me,' said Victoria and Mary together.

'I'll come with you, Father,' said Wilfred.

In the dining room the waiters were trying to lay tables. There were very few passengers to be seen.

'What's the damage like up top?' Henry asked a steward.

'Very untidy, sir. A spar broke on one of the masts in the night and caused a lot of damage. There are ropes and sails everywhere and the kitchen area has been partly demolished. So it's a cold breakfast, and lunch as well, I expect, sir.'

The wind blew all that day. As evening approached the heavy seas became calmer. Within an hour, the evening sun was shining through, and the sea seemed comparatively smooth. It was as if nothing had happened.

They were approaching Singapore, where the ship was due to call for re-provisioning. The captain announced that the ship would stay for five days instead of the scheduled two days.

On deck, Henry and Mary found that part of the deck had been cordoned off.

'What a night, wasn't it?' said Henry, to a man and woman of similar age to them who were viewing the damage of the night before.

'Yes; we didn't sleep a wink. Wendy kept thinking the boat would sink. We don't want many more nights like that. Are you going far?'

'Yes, we're going to our sheep farm in Australia. How about you?'

'We're getting off at Singapore. We have a house there and a small plantation. My name is Michael Harptree and this is my sister, Wendy.'

Henry introduced Mary and Victoria, who had just arrived on deck looking as green as the sea.

'We were just going into the lounge for a glass of beer. Would you like to join us?' asked Michael.

Henry looked at Mary for confirmation. 'Yes, thank you; lead on.'

They found a table and ordered drinks while Victoria went off to find her friend. The men were discussing travel and the prices of goods at home, so Mary turned to the lady who had been introduced as Wendy.

'Please excuse my curiosity, but did I hear you are Michael's sister?'

'Yes, that's right. I was until recently an Anglican nun, but I have finished my time with them and am coming home to lead a slightly more normal life.' She smiled.

'Yes, I understand. I was in Crimea with some Anglican nuns. They were very hard and conscientious workers. I admired them greatly.'

'I was in Crimea as well. I came out in March, 1855.'

'That was the month I came home,' Mary said.

'I don't suppose your name was Mary Langford, was it?'

Mary smiled. 'Yes, that was my name in those days. I have married and remarried since then.'

'Oh, I am pleased to meet you. Miss Nightingale has been a wonderful leader, and I am not taking anything away from her when I say that in Sevastopol Hospital you are a legend. They think the world of you.'

'That's very kind. Thank you, Wendy.' Mary sipped her drink. 'What do you intend to do now you are no longer a nun?'

'I think I would like to look after the poor and sick of Ceylon.'

'That's certainly commendable,' said Mary.

'Come on, ladies, let's have some more drinks,' said Michael.

'Not for me, Michael, thank you. I still have my fruit juice,' said Mary.

'What shall we drink a toast to?' asked Michael, raising his newly-charged glass.

'Let's drink to the future,' said Henry, and they all raised their glasses.

The passengers were allowed to disembark at ten the next day. Michael insisted they all come to his villa for drinks and lunch. Henry accepted reluctantly, though Mary and the children were in favour of the idea. A carriage was already waiting, with Michael and Wendy seated in it, when Henry and his family disembarked.

'Come on, Charlie,' said Michael, to the Chinese driver of their carriage. 'I'm gasping for a chilled bottle of champers. Eh, what say you?' He slapped Mary lightly on the knee.

They drove high up into the hills to a magnificent little hideaway villa, surrounded by palms and equatorial greenery which kept the scorching sun off the house.

'What's the big pool of water for?' asked Henry.

'That, my friend, is for us to lie in and cool off.'

'What a wonderful idea. What do you wear?'

'Well, it depends who I'm with. If it's a pretty maiden, then hardly anything.' He chuckled loudly. Wendy blushed. Mary, though, quite approved of the idea and wished she could strip to her bare essentials and lie in the pool, which was only about eighteen inches deep.

Lunch was lobster and crayfish salad, with sliced oranges in brandy. All of this was consumed with chilled champagne. The children took their socks off and paddled. They loved it.

Michael disappeared after lunch, saying he was going to get a cigar and some pictures to show them. They waited nearly forty minutes, but there was no sign of him.

'Whatever could have happened?' Wendy asked, agitated.

'Wait here and I will go and look for him,' said Henry.

'Michael,' he called, as he made his way through the villa. 'Mike... are you all right? Oh, my godfathers!' he exclaimed in horror. Michael was lying quite still in the hallway. Evidently the drink had caught up with him and urgent medical attention was needed, if he was not to die within minutes.

'Mary! Come quickly! Wendy! He's unconscious.'

Mary hurried to Michael's side and found his pulse, then checked to see whether he was breathing. She leaned over him and, placing her mouth over his, she blew.

Wendy grabbed her collar. 'What do you think you are doing? He needs help, not affection. This is no time to kiss my brother when he can't help himself,' she said, annoyed.

'I'm not kissing him. I am blowing air into his lungs, hoping to get him breathing again.' She tried again and again, keeping it up for ten minutes.

They all stood around in silence, convinced that Michael was dead and that Mary was wasting her time with this strange cure she was practising. Suddenly, he coughed and opened his eyes.

They all cheered.

'Where am I?' he asked.

'Lie still, we will get a doctor.'

'I don't need a—'

'Lie still. You nearly died. In fact you may have done,' said Mary sternly.

'Where on earth did you learn to blow into someone like that?' asked Henry. The two children stood looking on, amazed.

'In Crimea there was this young soldier. He just passed out and stopped breathing. Normally they would have taken him out and buried him. God knows how many might have been buried when they were not actually dead. Anyway, this boy looked so young and helpless. So I pushed the orderlies aside, opened his mouth and blew like I did then. After five minutes he recovered consciousness. Everyone was amazed. The military said it was witchcraft. They forbade me to ever do it again.'

'Where did you find out how to do it?

'To be honest, it was partly witchcraft. You see, when I was studying to be a nurse for Crimea I read everything I could find. One of the journals was *Medicines of Tribal Africa*. Most of the contents were beyond my comprehension, but I distinctly remembered reading about how they brought this girl back to life after she drowned in a river. I had never tried it before.'

Michael was sitting up now. Colour had returned to his cheeks. He wanted to get up, but Henry wouldn't let him.

'You owe your life to Mary,' said Wendy.

'I know. I'm eternally grateful, Mary. Thank the Lord you were here. How can I repay you?'

'By reducing your drinking and taking life a lot easier. That's how you can repay me,' she said with a smile.

The doctor, when he arrived, gave the patient a dose of laudanum and sent him to bed to rest for a few days. Mary and the family returned to the ship, leaving Wendy to look after her brother. Two days later the *Great Britain* continued her voyage to Australia.

There were ten single ladies on the ship going to Australia. The majority of these ladies were under forty years of age, and one or two of them were in their early twenties, so there was quite a mixture. Generally speaking, they were attractive and nicely dressed. They had been placed in the care of the captain to ensure their safety and chastity. John wasn't responsible if their chastity wasn't intact because some of the ladies had been married previously. They had separate cabins, two to a cabin, and their bedrooms were segregated, though they were able to enjoy all the privileges of the first-class passenger, which indeed they were.

Nearly all of these ladies were travelling to Australia to marry wealthy single men, the majority of whom had made their fortunes in the gold fields or on farms with sheep and cattle. The men had seen pictures of these ladies in magazines sent over from England. It was up to the individual to contact the lady of his choice, and if both were happy with the arrangement the money was sent to England for her fare. These ladies were happy to give up their freedom in England, travel to Australia and marry the man who had paid their fare. This practice was not unusual. However, ten ladies was one of the largest consignments of future brides the captain had ever had to look after. It was the captain's job not only to ensure they had privacy, but to entertain them and see that they weren't lonely.

Captain John Gray was a happily married man. He had no intention or desire to seek the company of these ladies, other than to walk with them, sometimes with one on each arm. Sometimes they would play games with him such as draughts or whist. Sometimes the ladies made advances towards him. After all, he was a fine specimen of a man and they must have thought he would make a fine sleeping companion. It was fair to say that the history of these ladies was what they had revealed to the booking agency, and what they had done to make a living prior to their boat journey was their secret. Practically every lady had asked him to attend her wedding, and as their fathers weren't able to be there they wanted him to act in their fathers' role and give them away.

The dates for these marriages had been fixed beforehand, and they would be held pretty well as soon as the boat had docked. The menfolk desperately wanted the affection of their chosen ladies, and would discuss other aspects of their marriages later. On the other hand, the ladies wanted the security of the promised marriage before parting with their chastity.

Apart from a few more gales the rest of the journey to Australia was uneventful. Every day when they woke up the sun was shining.

'What a difference from England, Mother. It is warm and brilliantly sunny here, and in England when we left it was wet and cloudy,' said Wilfred, taking in all the sights of the harbour. 'They speak differently, too, don't they, Father, the Australian people?'

'Yes, son. They have a sort of twang to their words. I'm sure it won't be long before you're speaking like a native.'

Wilfred still had questions for his parents. 'And why do they call us poms? We are Englishmen.'

'I know, my dear, but they think of us as immigrants and the nearest rhyming word they can find is "pomegranate".'

'It doesn't rhyme, though, Mother.'

'Don't let it worry you, Wilfred. You will come across other and bigger differences and you must learn to accept them. Remember, this is their country; we are the visitors.'

'Are you packed ready to disembark, dear?' Henry asked.

'No, I'm not. I still have breakfast to finish yet. There's no hurry, is there?'

'No, but I don't want to hang around when we get into harbour. I have Alex waiting for us with a pony and trap.'

'Alex... you mean my Alex? My stepbrother, the man who tried to rob us when we lived in England?'

'The very same. He's a changed man now. He's the ranch foreman, and he can never do enough for me.'

'Does he know I am his sister and have married his boss, and that we are coming out here?'

'Yes, he does.'

'What's that, Mother?' asked Wilfred, seeing the excitement on his mother's face.

'You're going to meet my brother. He is your uncle Alex, and has come out to Australia to help Father with his sheep farm.'

Wilfred looked a little confused,

'I didn't know you had a brother.'

"Yes my son I have, but he's not my real brother. It's just that we both had the same father, but not the same mother. I imagine he is some kind of a step brother."

CHAPTER 5

They arrived at Melbourne Harbour two hours later. Wilfred looked down on the quayside at all the shouting and traffic. There were rifle-carrying soldiers dressed in red and white coats, with plumes in their hats. They looked very untidy and slovenly, lounging against stacks of bales, talking and smoking. Their rifles stood unguarded next to them as they chatted with their friends.

The soldiers were supervising a workforce of poor white wretches who were hardly clothed. Their ankles were shackled and they walked with a shuffle, heads bowed, as if all interest in life had been beaten out of them by the overseer's whip, which he generously applied to their bare backs. Many of them showed the scars of previous beatings. The overseer seemed to apply the whip despite a man doing his best to lift a heavy bale.

Although Wilfred was fascinated, it sickened him to see human beings being treated in this fashion. He wondered what sort of a country he had come to which allowed such atrocious activities. His father came and stood next to him, watching the traffic on the quayside.

'What is it, Father? Why are they beating those poor men? Look at the condition of them!'

'I know what you mean, Wilfred, but this has been going on for nearly 150 years. You must have heard talk of the shipping of convicts to Australia? Well, the practice of sending prisoners out here has stopped, but there are still convicts serving their time, and there will always be people who have done wrong, so we will always have convicts. They are better-treated now than years ago. There is nothing you can do about it. It's a way of life out here. Remember, we were the ones who sent these poor wretches to Australia for some very petty crimes,' said Henry. 'Now, come on downstairs and help your mother. We will be disembarking shortly.'

The chain gangs were coming on board to assist in getting the ship unloaded.

'Look, Father, there are small children running around dressed in rags. What are they doing?'

'Some of the prisoners have children. They lead the lives of convicts themselves, though they are not beaten. Once they are past ten they are expected to earn their keep and do simple jobs. On board this ship you will find them cleaning the accommodation.'

Wilfred couldn't believe that children were treated like that. 'I think it's shameful, Father. I really do.'

'That's the way it is, Wilfred. You can't change it, so don't try.'

The convicts had been unshackled for the purpose of going on board the *Great Britain* so they could manoeuvre around the narrow steps and staircases. Wilfred noted the female convicts with their children; some even had babies. He was amazed at what he had seen. It was unbelievable.

Deep in thought, he went downstairs to his family cabin. As he walked along the corridor he saw what appeared to be a mobile bag of rags enter a door marked *STORES*. He stood outside, wondering what he should do. He guessed it must be one of the child convicts.

As he stood there quietly, the store door opened a little and a frightened face peeped out. It was small, very dirty, and had long, unwashed curly hair, which must have been light brown once. Today it was covered in blood, dirt and sweat. The child stared back at him for what seemed ages, but was probably no more than three seconds. Without a word, it went back inside the store, pulling the door shut behind it.

Wilfred's curiosity was alerted now, so he pushed open the door and entered the darkened storeroom. There was a little light filtering through a vent in the roof and he could just make out the figure crouched in the corner. It was sobbing. It couldn't harm him, thought Wilfred, if it was crying, so he spoke.

'Don't cry. What's the matter? Who are you?' he whispered.

'Don't give me in, master. Please don't tell them I am here,' the little wretch said through sobs.

Poor boy, thought Wilfred pityingly. 'What's your name?' he asked, attempting to get closer to the boy.

'Rose Brooks.' The child wiped its nose on its arm.

'Rose? Then you're a girl? What's a girl doing here?'

'My father is a prisoner, so I have had to stay here with him,' she said, hardly audibly. 'I am trying to hide, to escape from this terrible prison. I have been here a year and don't think I will live two years. It's hell on earth. My dad says it's God's dustbin of humanity. Have you got a crust of bread, sir?'

'No, I haven't. How old are you, Rose?'

'Ten, sir,' she replied, wiping her eyes on her sleeve, and smudging her dirty face.

'Don't call me "sir". I am only four years older than you. My name is Wilfred. Wait here and I will see what I can do. Hide under those sacks in case anyone comes looking for you.' He peeked out the door. Seeing it was all clear, he let himself out and went to his cabin.

'Where have you been, Wilfred?' his mother asked, looking somewhat harassed. 'We have all been looking for you. There is a glass of milk, and some bread and meat and an apple for your lunch. Now, hurry and eat up; we have to be off the ship in half an hour.'

Dare he tell his mother about Rose? he wondered. It would be difficult to help the girl without telling her.

'Mother, don't be angry with me, but I have something to tell you.'

'Yes, dear, what is it?'

'I have found a poor wretch of a girl who is starving and a prisoner. She is trying to hide so she won't go back to prison. She is only ten, Mother, and she has been beaten. Can we help her? Please.'

His father was out of the cabin, seeing to the unloading of the household effects brought from England. Mary listened attentively. It took her no time to make the decision.

'Go and get her and bring her in here quickly. I have an idea.'

The passageway was still empty. Wilfred went into the store. 'Rose,' he whispered. Her head appeared from the pile of sacks. 'Come quickly; we are going to help you.'

She was hesitant at first, perhaps thinking it was a trap. Then, apparently deciding she had nothing to lose, she stood up. Wilfred took her clammy, soiled hand in his and opened the door a little. Two men were coming down the corridor.

'When I find the little bitch, I'll tan her arse for her,' said a burly sergeant with a wart on his nose. 'Search the empty cabins; she can't be far away.'

Once the pair had passed, Wilfred tugged urgently on her thin arm. He pulled her after him into his cabin.

'Mother, this is Rose,' he said. Mary looked at the little girl and immediately understood why Wilfred wanted to rescue her.

'We must waste no time, child. Do you want to come with us?' said Mary.

Rose hesitated. She knew these people would be in terrible trouble if they were found out helping a prisoner to escape. But escape was what she wanted. Besides, she wasn't a convict; it had been her parents who had been convicted, and her mother had been dead a year.

'Quickly, yes or no?'

'Yes... yes, please,' said Rose.

'All right,' said Mary. 'Now quickly, get washed, undress and face me. Wilfred, go on deck and tell Father what we're doing. Tell him he is to take Victoria off the ship and leave her with Alex, then come back here as fast as you can. Hurry!'

She gave the child Wilfred's lunch. She could see that she was famished. Rose crammed the food down her throat, starving hungry. Mary fetched scissors and swiftly trimmed Rose's hair. Next she gave the child a good washing, particularly all the skin that would be exposed. Already there had been a big transformation. Next, Mary sorted out a few of Victoria's clothes. Rose was a tall girl, and a pair of Victoria's shoes fitted her.

The change was unbelievable. Mary felt sure she could be smuggled off now. She didn't look like the same scruffy, dirty child Wilfred had brought in twenty minutes ago.

Wilfred ran all the way up on deck. There were soldiers and other men searching under sacks and boxes.

'What's the matter, Father?' he asked, though he had guessed.

'A young woman has escaped from the prison gang and they think she is hiding on board as a stowaway, hoping to get back to England.'

'That's impossible, Father.'

'I know, son, but people do the strangest things and take great risks when they are desperate.'

'Father, Mother wants you to take Victoria ashore and leave her with Alex. She wants to smuggle the girl they are looking for off the boat as one of our family.'

Henry didn't know what his son was talking about. 'What do you mean, son?'

Wilfred knew he had to tell his father quickly what had happened so far and what his mother intended to do.

'Impossible! Your mother's mad!' Henry blurted out in astonishment. He thought for a moment or two. Then he said to Wilfred, 'Come with me, son. I have an idea.'

The two of them hurried back to the cabin. Rose was sitting, very composed, on the bunk. Wilfred could hardly credit the difference in her appearance. She was, underneath that grimy exterior, a pretty girl.

'Wilfred's told you?' said Mary, seeing the look on Henry's face.

'Oh yes, he told me. What do you think you're doing? You can't interfere in the control of the state and the prisons, Mary.' He looked at Rose, who was already shedding tears at his outburst.

There was silence for a moment. Nobody knew quite what to do, and there were only five minutes left before they were to disembark.

'I've got it,' said Henry. 'The two girls should walk together, talking and laughing like sisters, not looking at the guards or anything else. You're just two happy sisters. Understand? Can you do it? I will be watching. Don't be afraid, just be natural. Have you another doll for Rose?'

Victoria took one out of her bag and gave it to her.

'Remember,' said Henry, 'we are just one happy family. All right, let's go, and may God watch over us.'

'Amen,' said Mary as they trooped up on deck. The bright afternoon sunshine caught the girls by surprise, so they shielded their eyes as they walked towards the gangplank; this helped to hide their faces.

'What about the luggage?' asked Mary, as she ushered the children along.

'Don't worry, that's all in hand. I have arranged for the luggage, apart from what we are carrying, to be delivered to the ranch. They have our address.'

Henry was well aware that someone could be suspicious as he had been seen with only one daughter, but on the other hand, he reasoned, who on earth would suspect a couple travelling first-class of absconding with a young prison girl, when they already had a family of their own? It was this thought that gave Henry the courage to face the officials lingering on deck watching the passengers disembarking. He deliberately stood in their line of sight so that he blocked the view of the passengers getting off the ship. He noted that the captain was not in sight.

'My! It's good to get back home to Australia! I have missed it,' he said to the two soldiers.

'Have you, sir? Welcome back. The tucker is better back here, ain't it?' All three laughed heartily.

'They're two fine girls you have there, to be sure,' said the overseer in his thick Belfast accent.

'Thank you, sir,' said Henry, watching his family approach the gangplank. 'And that would be three fine girls including their mother?' he suggested, with a wink and a smile.

The Irishman took a moment to grasp his meaning.

'Oh yes, to be sure. That's three altogether,' he confirmed with a chuckle.

'Excuse me, sir,' asked an officer, 'you wouldn't happen to have seen a girl, a convict girl? She would be dirty and in rags. She wasn't near your compartments, by any chance?'

'No, there was nobody of that description on the first-class deck.'

'No! Of course not. Good day, sir,' He saluted Henry, who was about to leave the ship and follow the family down the gangplank when suddenly there was a shouted command from a soldier watching the passengers.

'Hey! Wait a minute!' shouted a corporal, who had been paying attention to the passengers disembarking. 'You, madam, with the two girls. Stop where you are.'

Mary froze. The game was up and some astute soldier had spotted Rose for what she really was. To continue could mean arrest.

'Stop, girls,' she said, as slowly she turned towards the direction of the shout. The corporal was running towards her. Henry stood with his mouth open, unable to do anything.

As the soldier got near the girls he picked up something. The girls hadn't moved, though Rose had started to weep at the thought of being caught out.

'What is it, Corporal?' asked Mary, who, with her experience in Crimea, was used to the military rank and file.

'Excuse me, ma'am,' he said, taking Rose by the shoulder and turning her round to face him. 'Don't cry, little girl. I saw you drop your doll, so I picked it up for you.' He smiled.

'That's kind of you, Corporal,' said Mary. 'Say thank you, Charlotte.' She dared not used the child's real name.

Rose was no fool. She thanked the soldier, keeping her face pointed downwards.

'I have two girls of my own, ma'am, so I understand.' He smiled at them again, turned and returned to his post, leaving Mary with her stomach still somersaulting. She began to breathe more easily.

Henry went over to the soldier and, taking out his wallet, he thanked him and handed him a golden guinea, equivalent to a month's pay for the man. The corporal beamed a broad smile and thanked him. Wishing them all good day, Henry walked down the gangplank and joined the family, who were by now already seated in the carriage which was to take them to the farm.

'Take us home, Alex, and don't waste any time. We will explain later,' he said to the driver. Without a word, Alex cracked his whip and the carriage leapt on its way to the farm.

When they were well out of sight, Henry told Alex to stop. 'I think we have pulled that off successfully. Alex, this is your sister, Mary.'

'I know; I remember how beautiful she was. Hello, my dear sister.'

'Hello, Alex. It's lovely to see you,' said Mary, hugging him.

'And this little maid is Rose, who we have stolen out of prison without being detected,' said Henry.

They had barely started to drive again when an excited shout came from Wilfred. 'Father, look! There is a horseman galloping this way. He wants us to stop.'

Henry realised there was no use in trying to outrun the soldier on horseback. He had the carriage brought to a stop. The rider soon came up to them.

'Sir,' he said, out of breath, 'you left your purse on the ship. I was sent to give it to you.'

Henry was very relieved, as was everyone else in the carriage. 'That's very good of you, my man,' he said, handing the man a tip. 'Come on, family, not much further to the ranch. Carry on, driver.'

They all laughed and cheered with relief.

'Captain, we seem to have lost a little girl on your ship,' said the sergeant.

'What little girl? Do you mean one of my passengers' children is missing?' asked John, very concerned.

'No, Captain, she is the ten-year-old daughter of one of our prisoners who was put on board to help clean the cabins and we can't find her.'

John wasn't too bothered as long as it wasn't one of his passengers. 'All right, Sergeant. I will get the crew to give the ship a good search. How old did you say she was?'

'Ten, sir, and her name is Rose.'

John knew he couldn't waste any time as he had a wedding to attend in an hour. It was Miss Violet Hamish's. She was only twenty-one years old and had come out to Australia to marry Clarence Mills, a gold miner. He was forty-five years old.

A horse and carriage waited on the quayside.

'Hello!' said John. 'Are you waiting for me?'

'If your name is Captain Gray, then yes, I am. Climb aboard and I will take you to the wedding.'

The driver and John chatted away like old friends.

'Here we are, sir. Don't worry about the fare; it's all looked after.'

'Thank you,' said John. 'I hope we meet again.'

John walked over to where a group of men were standing dressed in their Sunday best. One man was pacing up and down nervously and looking at his watch. John guessed this must be the best man.

'Hello! Everything all right?'

The man turned and looked at him. 'No, it's not. The bride and groom are missing.'

'Don't worry, there's plenty of time. It's not unusual for them to be late. I'm here to give the bride away,' said John.

'Well, that's a relief; at least you're here.'

'My name is John Gray. I am the captain of the *Great Britain*.'

The man didn't seem impressed. 'Nice to meet you. I am Vic Mullins.' He checked his watch again.

'Here they come. I can hear them; they sound very happy,' said John, as the bridal carriage came into view. They both seemed a little tipsy and Violet was definitely looking the worse for wear.

'Captain Gray, you have made it. You have made my day.'

John took her hand and kissed it. 'The pleasure is all mine, Violet,' he said.

'This is my husband-to-be. His name is Clarence.'

Clarence smiled and took John's hand. 'I am honoured to make your acquaintance,' he said, with a strong handshake.

'Come on, everybody,' said Vic, 'the parson is waiting.' They all shuffled their way into the gloomy church hall where the guests were mostly the groom's friends.

The service didn't take long; John was sure the parson had left half of it out. Afterwards, they made their way on foot to a small hotel across the road; it was called the Ring of Bells, and was very comfortable. There were tables full of plenty of meats, pies, pastries and pickles. This was followed with a large selection of jelly and more pies, fruit and custards. John ate his fill and was very satisfied.

When it came time to leave he thanked his host and hostess. The band were playing, but John still had a lot to do, and he had another wedding to attend the next day. The men who were awaiting their new brides didn't waste any time in getting wed.

It was dark outside the hotel. There was a gas lamp nearby, but it did a poor job of lighting the street. A horse and carriage came up to the door. It wasn't the same one that had brought him to the wedding. This carriage driver was old and bent and kept his face covered.

'Will you take me to the *Great Britain*, which is docked on quay nine?' asked John.

'All right. Get on board.'

John climbed aboard and settled down. The carriage shot off at a sharp pace. John was thrown back in his seat.

'Hey. Steady on. There's plenty of time.'

The driver ignored John's request, and drove a route out of town that John was not familiar with.

'Stop, sir! This minute!' shouted John. But the driver ignored him and used his whip on his horse to make it go faster. John grabbed the man by the throat. The carriage was going too fast to allow John to jump off. The horse had been given its order and didn't want another whip lash. The carriage bounced all over the place as they were in the countryside.

Suddenly the driver pulled the horse to a halt outside a lonely house standing on its own. It was very dark. Two men came out of the house and without a word frogmarched John into the house, where they put manacles on both his wrists.

'What are you doing? Let me go. Who are you?'

They said nothing, and left the room.

The room was lit by a single candle. There was a bed with one blanket and a pillow, a toilet bucket and a chair. John's chains enabled him to reach all of these as required. He sat on the chair, wondering what he had done to deserve this. Nobody came to see him. He was left alone. He found a replacement candle; there was nothing else. He called out for some time but nobody came.

In the end he lay on the bed, wondering why someone had done this to him. It had obviously all been carefully planned and the room prepared with what his captors knew he needed as basic essentials. What was the motive, he wondered, and who was responsible? They certainly hadn't wasted any time.

Eventually, he dropped off to sleep. A very bad headache woke him up, and his guts were aching. He relieved himself and felt a little better. Daylight was filtering through the single mucky window, which had a crack down the middle of it. The room stank of pigs, though John was used to this.

A man entered the room and set down a tray with a lump of bread and a jug of water. It was put just out of John's reach, so that he had to stretch out and move the tray towards himself by dragging it with his feet. He didn't feel like eating. The man's face was hidden by a mask. He didn't say anything and did not answer John's questions as to where he was and why he was here.

When the man had left, John lay back on the bed wondering about his ship, and if they were missing him and wondering where he was. The first and second mate were quite capable of seeing to the ship and the repairs it needed. It was quite likely they thought he was enjoying the wedding he had gone to. They knew by his diary that he had another wedding to attend the following day, so they wouldn't miss him. There was nothing he could do about it. He lay back on his stinking pillow and tried to sleep.

The first sign that anything was wrong was when the intended bridegroom of Rose Woolsey sent a messenger to the ship to say that the bridal couple were waiting at the church for John to show up as he had promised to give her away. The officers knew only too well that their captain would not let anyone down and would ensure they were informed if he found himself unable to attend. They started making enquiries to see if they could find where he was.

The following day the first officer for the return journey, Mr Chapman, was handed a letter which said the captain was alive and well and he would be released for £500. The officers now knew that John was being held hostage, but not where. The police were called in and every effort was made to find out where he was being held captive.

On the third day of John's imprisonment, a man appeared at his door.

'Hello, Captain Gray. Are you well? How do you like being shackled in a pigsty, and fed on bread and water? That's what you do to passengers on your ship who you think have misbehaved. It's not very nice, is it? This is the nearest we can get to what you put us through. Now, all we want is for your ship to pay 500 guineas and we will release you.' He laughed, and left the room.

John hadn't recognised the man. He had worn a false beard and a cap pulled over his eyes.

John lay back, thinking. He felt sure his officers would know of the ransom, but he knew that, having paid the Egyptian police, there was little money left in the purser's safe.

The enquiries about John's disappearance were starting to yield answers. It seemed that John had caught the wrong coach from the hotel that night. He should have been taken back to the ship by the same carriage that had taken him to the wedding. Apparently, his intended driver had been given a false call which meant he would be late. The people who had set the trap up had enlisted the help of an old man, giving him triple the fare to pick John up and take him to the house where he had been imprisoned. The old driver was known locally as Dirty George.

Two young boys called at the police station the following day and said they had found a man dead down by the water, and his horse was there as well. The animal was all right and was busy munching grass. The policemen thanked the lads and took them to show where the man was to be found.

'It's Dirty George, the cab man,' the constable said. 'He looks dead. I wonder what killed him.'

'Or who,' said his sergeant, turning the body over. 'It's a bad bash on the head that has done it. He has been hit with something very heavy. I wonder why. It can't be for the little money he carried. Ask around the other carriage drivers and see if we can come up with something.'

'I think he died and took his secrets with him, Sergeant,' said the constable.

'Never mind what you think; go and make enquiries.'

'Yes, Sergeant,' he replied.

There was a big write-up in the local paper that night; it offered a £200 reward for information leading to the safe return of John Gray.

The bearded man came back to see John that evening.

'You are headlines, Captain. It's on the front page of the daily newspaper.' He tossed the paper on John's bed. John read it through.

'I don't think we will be able to raise all that money for my release. What happens then?' asked John.

'If that is the case, then we will kill you. It's as simple as that.'

Chapter 6

Sam and his two nephews Bob and Jim arrived at the mine sharp on nine o'clock. Their neighbours' mine was already hard at work. Sam had taken the boys to the store to buy all he thought they would need at this stage of the operations. Their purchases included dynamite and picks and shovels.

'You boys new here?' the storekeeper had asked. He was a short, tubby man with a bald head. 'My name is Sidney and this is my daughter Emilee.'

A beautiful girl came and stood by his side. She obviously took after her mother for good looks.

'How do you do, Emilee?' said Bob, with a big friendly smile at her.

'Yes, we are new boys to the mining trade. I know we've got lots to learn. These are my nephews, who came over from England only yesterday,' said Sam.

'My, you haven't wasted much time in getting started.'

Emilee didn't say anything but gave them a smile. Bob was very taken by her and kept trying to catch her eye. He thought she was the most beautiful woman he had ever met. She was about five foot four, with auburn hair and blue eyes. She certainly looked out of place out here in the shanty mining town.

'Do you come from England, Emilee?' he asked her. It seemed one way of breaking the ice between them.

'No, I was born in Australia. I came out here with my parents and am helping them run the family business,' she said, coyly.

'Glad to make your acquaintance, Emilee,' he said, touching his hat as the three men left the store.

'My, you were really taken by her, Bob,' said Sam.

'I thought she was gorgeous,' said Bob.

'You've been away from English girls too long,' said Jim.

'Plenty of time for romance once your pockets are full of gold,' said Sam. Bob said nothing, but he was determined to get back to the store at the first opportunity to see Emilee. They mounted their horses and trotted over to where their mine was.

Bertie was standing outside the mine, lighting his pipe.

'Good morning. I see you've been to the store and brought plenty of gear with you. Did you catch sight of that pretty daughter of his? I reckon every man here has an eye on catching her as a bride.'

'Yes,' said Bob. 'She sure is very beautiful.'

'Right! Let's have a look at the mine and where we intend to make our opening blast.'

The four men looked at the hillside from different angles and eventually agreed it should be attacked from the south face. They marked out the area where they wanted the mouth of the mine to be and set about knocking boreholes in the rock, ready for the dynamite. It was hard work, and the tenderfoot miners were soon pissing on their blistered hands to harden the skin. This was the recognised way of toughening skin.

It was mid-afternoon before all the boreholes were finished. Sam didn't work on the excavation of the mine, but busied himself with lighter tasks.

'OK, stand right back. I'm going to light the fuse,' said Bertie.

They all ran for cover and waited for the big bang. When it went off, there were rocks and debris blown everywhere.

'Cover your faces till the dust settles,' yelled Bertie. 'Don't let it get in your lungs or you will be coughing for ever. You will meet a lot of old miners who learnt that the hard way.'

Jim rushed forward after the dust had settled, and started picking up rocks.

'What are you doing, little brother?' asked Bob.

'Searching for gold,' said Jim, excitedly.

'Don't be so keen. It will be weeks before you catch sight of any, and even then you will be lucky.'

'What do you mean, Bertie?' asked Bob.

'Well, there is many a mine opened up that never yields any gold. They're called barren maidens.'

'Well, I didn't know that,' said Sam.

'Not saying yours is going to be like that, but just be aware it could be.'

They set to clearing the mouth of the cave they had created.

'What's next, Bertie?' asked Bob.

'We do the same thing again. Then we will have to shore it up with planks of wood you can get from the store.'

'It's starting to get dark and I think you boys deserve a meal and a few beers,' said Sam. 'What say you, Bertie?'

'I reckon you're right. You have worked hard today. See you in the pub,' said Bertie.

Bob called into the store, hoping to catch a glimpse of Emilee. Her father Sidney was serving.

'What can I do for you?' he asked, half-guessing Bob's real reason for being there.

'I, I, I was wondering if you have any planks for shoring up the mine,' said Bob.

'There's a big pile over there and a big sign outside saying so. Now tell me what you really came for.'

Bob was taken aback, and had to stop to think. 'Nothing, nothing at all.'

'Sure? It wasn't to see Emilee, was it?'

'No! Well, yes, I would like to speak to her if she's not busy,' said Bob.

Emilee didn't need calling; she came into the shop. She smiled at Bob, who returned her smile.

'I think this gentleman has called to see you, Emilee. Keep an eye on the store; I have to go into the lounge for some papers,' said her father, winking at Bob as he left them alone.

'Can I help you, sir?' she asked.

'My name is Bob and I think you are the most beautiful girl in the world. Would you walk with me this evening?'

'My parents won't allow me to walk alone. Would you like to come here and talk to me?'

'Indeed I would. Can I come at eight?'

'Yes, that would be fine. I look forward to seeing you,' she said, with a smile.

Bob left the store feeling as if he had struck a vein of gold. He felt so happy. He didn't say anything to his family about his date that evening, but made some excuse that he wanted to get some fresh air, alone.

Emilee's family were waiting for him when he called.

'Come into the main room and sit down. Can I get you a drink?' asked Sidney. He introduced his wife as Grace. She didn't work the store as she had lumbago, and spent most of her time sitting down making bed covers, which they sold in the store.

'Do you like it here, Emilee?' asked Bob.

'It's all right, but I want to travel and see the world. I would love to go to England one day,' she said. 'Where do you live in England, Bob?'

He told her where they lived and about his mother, and the story of how they had come to be in Australia.

'So this is an adventure for you,' said Sidney, who had been listening in.

'Yes, very much so. I don't know if we will find any gold or not, but I must return to England one day as I have a lot of friends who invested in my gold mine.'

'What do you mean?' asked Grace.

'I sold shares at two pounds each to finance our trip.'

'Very enterprising,' said Sidney. 'I think you will make a good businessman.' All three agreed with him.

The conversation that followed was mainly small talk, hobbies and other interests, just getting to know each other. He only stayed an hour but felt he had made friends with the family, though it was Emilee who asked him to come back soon. He shook hands with her parents, and took Emilee's hand and kissed it as he wished her goodnight.

The next day, back at the mine, work started again, only this time they were shown what to look for in the rocks which would promise a vein of gold ore. Both brothers were excited and hardly left a stone unturned, but found no gold ore. They were using their pickaxes and shovels. Bertie called round now and again to advise them. They had bought the boarding planks to secure the roof and prevent it from falling in.

Bob felt it was time to tell his family that he had made advances to Emilee and was hoping it would develop into a love affair and eventually marriage. They congratulated him and wished him luck.

Every day they worked at the mine and progressed more and more into the hillside. A week went past, and there was still no sign of gold. The brothers were getting a little despondent; it was all work and no pay. They were now three yards into the hillside.

'You should be hitting gold dust soon,' said Bertie. 'Don't lose heart. It took me nearly three weeks before I found any, and even then I could hardly see it because it was so small. Keep at it, boys.'

That evening, Sam, Bob and Jim went over to the bar for a drink and to listen to the singer who was entertaining. It was a busy evening and there were plenty of patrons enjoying the atmosphere. Sam and his crowd were known by most of the regulars because what Sam had done, that night when Bertie had been threatened, could have saved a man's life. The accuracy of his shooting had ensured the criminal hadn't died, but he wouldn't be using that gun hand for a long time.

A man staggered up to their table. He appeared to be the same age as Bob.

'Ah, there you are, you pommy bastard,' he yelled out. 'I hear you been chatting up my Sheila.'

Bob ignored the drunk.

'Well, you got anything to say?' said the drunk.

'Nope,' said Bob.

'Well, I want to fight you for her. A fist fight. Are you on?' he shouted.

'I would rather not fight you.'

'Why not?'

'Because I don't want to take advantage of a drunk.'

'Don't call me a drunk. Come on, stand up and fight.' He staggered and rocked the table; glasses full of ale fell over, splashing them all.

'I think it's best if you put him to sleep,' said Jim.

Bob knew what his brother meant. Bob had been a professional fighter in his time. He reluctantly stood up. The crowd in the bar, sensing a good fist fight, formed a circle and pushed the two men into the centre. Bob went to take his jacket off, and as he did so the man socked him hard on the chin. It was an unfair blow, but Bob knew this fight wouldn't be by Queensbury rules, but rules of the jungle. A method he was not familiar with.

The ruffian swung punches wildly. Bob ducked, weaved and sidestepped, constantly jabbing with his left and scoring hits. He gave the man some sharp body blows which slowed him up. Then, catching him off balance, he landed a beautiful left hook which put him down and out for the count of ten.

Bob was wildly cheered by the crowd. Somebody came over with a jug of water and poured it over the man on the floor. The man spluttered, and walked away feeling foolish and disgruntled.

'Come on, boys, let's get out of here,' said Sam, finishing his beer and rising to his feet.

The next day it was the same routine at the mine, but they were making progress.

'Look here, Bob,' said Bertie, handing him a lump of rock.

'What am I looking for?' asked Bob.

'That shiny golden speck: that's gold, and it's from your mine.'

Bob's face lit up. 'Hey, Jim, come and have a look at our gold.'

Sam stood there smiling; understandably the boys were excited.

'Come on,' said Jim, 'let's do some more digging,' and the pair of them got stuck in with their pickaxes. They started to find more and more bits of gold.

'Keep looking, boys; you're trying to find the main seam. It will appear as a long shiny strip of yellow. Make sure you get all of it.'

Nothing could stop the boys now that they had gold fever. By the end of the day they had accumulated quite a pile of rocks with gold in each of them.

'What do we do with these?' asked Bob.

'You take them over to the assay office, who will weigh them and tell you how many grams you have. Don't set your hopes high. We are talking of only a few grams,' said Bertie.

'What, from all that rock?' asked Jim.

'I'm afraid so; most of what you got there is just rock,' he said, with a wink at Sam.

Bob came out the assay office with a big grin.

'We got fifty grams of gold and the man said it was top quality.' He let out a 'Whoopee!'

'That's something you mustn't do, is shout about your claim. There's people here just waiting to claim-jump. Make everyone think you're struggling,' said Bertie.

'Right! Sorry about that. You got the message, Jim?'

Jim nodded, to say he understood.

Every day their pile of rocks got bigger and the assay value went up. They still hadn't hit the main seam, but it didn't dampen their spirits; they just kept on digging.

Bob called regularly on Emilee. She laughed when she heard how he had defended her honour and reputation.

'Poor Tony,' she said. 'He tried so hard to be my escort, but his breath smells and he drinks all the time. Not the sort of man I want to marry.'

'I hope I fit the bill,' said Bob.

'Well, you're doing all right. I will let you know,' she said with a smile.

'Have you read the Gold Rag News?'

'No, whats that?' asked Bob.

'It's the local gold mine news paper.'

'I haven't told you before but I can't read or write.'

'Goodness me, would you like me to teach you?'

'Yes, I would be delighted if you would.'

'Right, we will start tomorrow,' she said with a smile.

Bob hadn't kissed her yet, or been allowed to spend more than a few minutes with her alone. He was certain she was the girl for him.

'My parents suggested you might like to come to dinner,' said Emilee.

'That's fine. I'd like to, but I only have the clothes I stand up in.'

'Come into the store, and I will sort some clothes out for you.'

Bob followed her. She guessed his size, and within no time he was dressed and looked very smart.

'My!' she said. 'What a difference. That's how I want my husband to dress.'

Bob was pleased he had made a good impression on her.

He went for dinner two nights later, dressed in his new clothes. By now he had been accepted and passed the scrutiny of Emilee's parents. They had taken to him and were encouraging the romance between the two.

'May I be permitted to walk with Emilee, just a stroll together one evening?' Even out here in the outback of Australia there were still many people whose way of life wasn't much different from those back in England.

'Would you like that, Emilee?' asked her father.

'Yes, Father, I would,' she replied. Emilee's mum grasped her hand to show she was pleased.

'Bob, you are welcome to walk with Emilee,' said her father.

'Thank you both,' he said, with a big grin to his blushing lady friend. 'Shall we go for a walk tomorrow?'

'If it's not raining,' she said.

'OK, see you tomorrow,' said Bob.

Bob and Jim continued working on the mine, and one afternoon when they were both feeling very tired, Bob gave the rock face a final blow and the rock fell away. He couldn't believe his eyes when he saw a line of gold two inches wide and two feet long. He gulped. Jim came over to see what he was staring at.

'That's it, Bob, that's the seam we've been looking for,' said Jim. 'Shall we start digging it out now?'

'Yes, let's make a start.'

The two of them picked away, making sure that every piece was carefully removed. The seam was deep and it was pure gold. Neither said a word. They gathered up what they had and closed the seam so anyone entering the mine wouldn't see it.

'What shall we do with this gold, Bob?'

'Let's take it to the assay office right away,' he said.

The assay man was pleased to see them. 'You have found a good seam. Here is a receipt; come and get the cash in the morning.'

They left the office feeling as if they were on cloud seven.

That night Bob took Emilee for a walk. He didn't tell her of the seam they had uncovered. He wanted to keep it quiet. Bertie had warned him of the dangers of people knowing what was being produced in the mine.

Sam was told of the find and he was nearly as excited as the brothers. Bob could hardly sleep with excitement; he kept on thinking of Emilee and the gold find. He was glad when morning came and they could continue digging gold.

When they arrived at the mine in the morning they found that the mine and the gold had been raided in the night. Somebody had taken the whole seam. How much money had they lost? Well, one could only guess. All their hard work had been pillaged in the night. Even their tools had been taken. It was usual on a site like this that one trusted one's fellow miners. Bob and Jim were much deflated, and were ready to throw their hand in.

'Don't worry about it, boys; these things happen out here in the bush. Just make sure your mine is secure. Sleep out here,' said Bertie.

'You can have my gun if you decide to sleep at the mine,' said Sam.

'You can have the use of my rifle as well,' said Bertie.

'We have never fired a gun,' said the boys.

'OK, we will teach you this afternoon. You won't be crack shots, but at least you will know which end to point at the person you're going to shoot.' They all laughed at Bertie's humour.

That afternoon the four of them went on some scrubland and Sam set up some beer bottles as targets. Bertie showed the boys how to load and fire his rifle. Both the brothers seem to take to the firearms as if they were used to it. Despite careful coaching and firing in the prone position they didn't actually hit a bottle, but came within inches of doing so. They tried kneeling and standing positions, but found they were wandering all over the place. Next it was Sam's turn to show them how to use the pistol. It was Jim who took to this weapon. He found he could shoot with accuracy and burst two of the bottles at ten feet.

'Don't worry about a quick draw from the holster. Just concentrate on lining the pistol up with the target and gently squeeze the trigger; don't snatch it,' said Sam. He gave them a demonstration of his own skill with the pistol and burst every bottle with one shot each.

'You must have spent a hell of an amount of time practising to shoot like that,' said Bertie, who was very impressed.

Sam holstered his gun. 'Yes, I do a lot of practice at home. It's a kind of hobby. Come on then, lads; that is enough for today.'

They went back to the mine and spent another two hours hacking away at the mine's rock face. There was no trace of another gold seam. Bob went and collected the money from the assay office and put it straight into their account.

That night, when it was dark, the brothers returned to the mine and tried to make themselves comfortable on the rock-strewn floor. They had managed to buy some blankets and pillows from the store. Bob was continually meeting up with Emilee, and was now treated as a friend of the family.

It had been on their fourth evening of walking out that there had been any significant advancement in Bob and Emilee's relationship. It was Emilee who took Bob's hand first. Bob was secretly delighted at this improvement in their relationship. Because of this the pair of them became much closer, till one moonlit night he kissed her. She responded instantly; it was as if she had been waiting for it to happen. One kiss soon turned into lots of kisses.

Bob was so elated at their progress that he had the courage to tell her he loved her. She didn't respond to the word of affection; she wanted to be sure. She did like Bob a hell of a lot, and felt she loved him. He had all the qualities a girl could hope to find in a man. Plus, he stood out amongst all the other contenders on the site, of whom there were over 200. She was used to their wolf-whistles and glances, and was continually turning down invitations to go out. Eventually, word got around that she was Bob's girl and the invitations dropped off. After all, Bob had gained his reputation of 'man with the iron fist', and had proved it in the bar that night.

Emilee was very concerned when Bob told her of the theft of gold from the mine; in fact she was shocked. She had never supposed such mean, deceitful actions took place amongst the brotherhood of gold miners.

Bob took her to the beer house one afternoon. He was careful to ensure that there were no hooligans present. They had a drink but didn't stay long. It really was intended as somewhere else to go. There was very little in the way of variety or entertainment.

'Can you play whist?' asked Emilee, another afternoon.

'No, I have seen it played. Can you play?'

'Yes. Sit down and I will show you.'

He had played poker plenty of times, so he knew what the cards were, and their seniority. After a few minutes he had the hang of it and was enjoying a game with her.

'Come round this evening, Bob, and we will make a foursome up, playing against my parents.'

He went and played the game, and at ten he said he had to leave as he and his brother were sleeping in the mine, and had been all week. Emilee and her parents were shocked to hear that they had been sleeping in the mine, and offered them two mattresses which, although they weren't thick, would be a lot more comfortable than lying on the ground.

A week went by; nothing happened. The boys had grown used to sleeping rough, and once or twice had wakened in the night thinking that someone had entered the cave.

'Let's spread a rumour that we have found another seam; perhaps it will make our gold robbers try their hand at stealing gold which isn't there,' said Jim.

'I agree, but we must keep secret what we are planning to do. Only those very close to us can be told of what we are doing, and even then they must be trustworthy. I suggest Sam and Bertie, not his labourers, and Sidney, Emilee's dad. He can start the rumour off for us. I think it will be a good idea, particularly if we can get our gold back. I think it is still on-site somewhere,' said Bob.

He told Sam of their plan; they knew he wouldn't say anything.

'Shall we tell Bertie?' asked Bob.

'No; the less that know, the better,' said Sam.

Bob went over to the store. There were many customers browsing items in the store. Bob saw Sidney and called him over. 'We found a big seam yesterday in our mine; that's the second one in a month. We will have to make sure no one pinches this one.' He winked at Sidney to imply it was only a hoax, and elaborated on the lie later when the store was empty.

Emilee came into the store; she must have heard Bob's voice. She came over smiling and gave him a kiss. This was the first time her father had seen them do this, but he must have realised they were very close, and possibly in love.

'What are you doing, my love?' Emilee asked, looking Bob straight in the eye.

He put his arm round her waist. 'I was hoping to see you, my sweetheart,' he responded.

'Is that all?' she asked, pretending to be disappointed.

'To me it is the most important incentive I could have. Having seen you I feel I can go and do a good day's work trying to earn money for our future.'

'I am glad to see you are thinking positively,' she replied, kissing him once more with her moist, tender lips. 'See you tonight, my dear. Do you want to bring your brother over as well?'

'No, thanks for the offer, but I want you to myself.'

Sidney ducked his head under the counter and grinned. He had never heard the two of them talking like that. He knew he had to tell his wife what he had overheard.

Bob and Jim were busy again that day digging in the mine. They found more gold, but it was only the tail end of the seam they had lost.

'I've been thinking,' said Bob. 'I think it would be a good idea if we don't sleep in the mine tonight, but close by, and we make up two lookalike bodies in the cave. That way we can take it in turns to sleep and at the same time see if anyone enters the mine.'

'No, I don't agree. If the thieves go in the mine and find sleeping dummies they will know that they are in a trap and will leave. It's better we leave the cave empty and watch from a distance,' said Jim.

'Yes,' said Bob, 'I believe you're right. That sounds a good idea. Also I think we should remove our tools to where we are sleeping so that the thieves can't use them.'

'Right, Bob. We will do that,' said Jim.

They didn't tell a soul what they intended to do, but once the darkness set in and the miners left to get their evening meal, Bob and his brother set about play-acting that they were sleeping in the mine. They had made sure that the lie about having found gold had been well circulated.

'Look, Bob, here is a mound we can hide behind. We can't be seen from the mine but we can still see what's going on.'

'Right, Jim, this is where we will make our base camp. Of course you realise that they may not come tonight and we will have lost a night's sleep.'

'I know, but I feel they will come and try to steal our gold tonight.'

It was cold at night. The boys felt it, being outside in the dark. They were fortunate that there was a full moon that night. They were each keeping watch in turn, two hours on and two off.

Jim was on duty. He checked his watch; it was 2.30 in the morning. He yawned. He had another half-hour to go before shaking his brother awake. Suddenly he saw three men entering their cave. He woke his brother.

'They have gone in,' he whispered.

'OK, pick up a gun and follow me,' said Bob.

They approached the mine from the side. The thieves had set up some candles and were already searching for the gold seam.

'Right, you gold robbers, put up your hands,' said Bob. Jim was beside him, holding a cocked pistol. One man, whose face they couldn't see, picked up a rifle as if to fire it. Jim fired first. The bullet hit the man high up in his right chest.

'Drop your pistols and rifles,' yelled Bob. The little shanty town had a sheriff and a jail, and that was where they intended to take the robbers.

'I don't believe it. These robbers are from the mine next door,' said Jim.

'The one we shot is Bertie. I thought you were our friend, not a gold robber,' said Bob.

Sam appeared at the mouth of the mine. 'I heard the shot and guessed it came from here. Bertie, what are you doing here? Robbing our mine?'

The other two men with Bertie were his mine workers.

'Remember I told you we were robbed some time ago?' Bertie asked, clutching his chest. 'Well, we have just found another seam of gold, but it runs into your mine, not ours. When we heard you had found a seam we thought that must be it, so we came to take what we thought was ours.'

'That's a bloody weak excuse. What about the gold we had taken? Was that you as well?'

'No. Well, not directly. It was Skirty and Shirty, my two helpers,' said Bertie.

'Where is that gold now?' asked Sam.

'In a crate, in our mine,' said Bertie.

'I'm ashamed of you, Bertie, robbing us,' said Sam.

'Our mine is useless now. We won't find any more. You have a new seam to work. I didn't tell my men to rob you, but I didn't stop them either.'

'Right, I want that gold back here right away,' said Sam. 'Bob, take the rifle with you. Get the gold and bring it back here. Bertie's men will assist you.'

It took an hour to shift it back to Sam's gold mine, because it was so heavy.

'Right, I will stay here and keep an eye on the gold. Bob and Jim, take these men to the jail.'

'We're taking you to jail, Bertie, all three of you,' said Jim.

'Get going, and don't try and run or we will shoot you,' added Bob.

Chapter 7

'How long will it take us to get to the sheep farm, Father?' asked Wilfred.

'About an hour,' Henry replied. He laughed. 'I see Alex has brought food and water with him. You can see I have trained him well.'

'Rose, I haven't introduced you to your new family,' said Mary. 'Would you like to refer to us as Mother and Father? I know you had your own once, but we will be your new parents, and these will be your brother and sister, Wilfred and Victoria.'

'Oh yes, Mother, I would like that. I can't thank you all enough for your bravery in rescuing me from the jail. My mother died a year ago and my father, who was convicted with her, is still serving time. They kept me in the prison even though I had done no wrong. My parents stole a sheep. We were starving and nearly dying. They both got twenty-five years. My father is getting very old and weak. I don't know how much longer he will last.'

'Will he worry about you, Rose?'

'Will you write him a letter telling him all he needs to know, Mother?'

'Of course I will, dear,' said Mary.

'I can't get over the way we stole Rose away from them, right under their noses,' said Victoria.

'It was done so quickly, Mother, wasn't it?' added Wilfred.

'I think that's the secret,' said Henry. 'It was the sheer audacity of the snatch. Nobody suspected it could be done. It wasn't as if we knew the child.'

'So you're not really a prisoner at all, then, Rose?' asked Mary. 'This throws a different light on the subject. We haven't really committed a crime, as we certainly haven't kidnapped you.'

'It's good to know we haven't actually committed a crime, like rescuing a prisoner,' said Henry, feeling very relieved.

The whole party, including the two horses, were getting tired after their long drive across the scrubland. There was nothing to see for miles. Wilfred kept standing up in the cart, looking into the distance, whilst shading his eyes from the sun.

Suddenly he pointed into the distance. 'Is that the farm ahead of us?' he demanded.

'Yes, son, that's it. That's our sheep farm, and it's your new home.'

'What is it?' asked Rose.

'It's a sheep farm,' replied Wilfred.

'Remember, Wilfred, Rose hasn't had the chances you have had to see all the wonders of life,' said Mary. 'She's been locked in a prison.'

They drove into the sheep farm. The flocks of sheep seemed to stretch for miles; there were thousands of them. They entered a spacious courtyard with flower gardens on each side. A stone-built farmhouse with white walls faced them. It was two storeys high, with double windows on each side; three steps led up to a large studded door. The windows had coloured curtains hanging from them. The whole atmosphere was of home and comfort. Around the back were more buildings; these were for the staff who ran the sheep farm.

Mary was most impressed. 'Henry, you have done well. Have you done all this yourself?'

'With a little help from my friends,' he said, grinning at her. He was immensely proud of what he had done.

They all alighted from the wagon and were pleased to stretch their legs after the long journey.

'Can we go inside, Father?' asked Wilfred.

'Of course you can, son; it's your home now. See that lady over there? Well, she runs the house. Her name is Patsy. You can call her Patsy; she won't mind. If there's anything you need to know about the house, just ask her. She will show you around and where your rooms are.'

The three children ran whooping and yelling into the spacious farmhouse.

'As for you, Mrs Harper, I am going to carry you over the threshold,' said Henry. With that he picked her up and they laughed together as they entered their new home.

The dining room was laid for a sumptuous dinner. As one might expect, roast lamb was on the menu, but the family were so hungry they all tucked in. Mary was knowledgeable enough to know that where Rose was concerned, the operative words regarding her intake of food would be 'little' and 'often'; she just was not used to it.

Mary was most taken, not only with the exterior, but with the interior of the house. As far as she could see, very little needed improvement. As the building was comparatively new, all the furniture was likewise.

Henry introduced the staff, who had lined up in the hall to greet them. The family moved down the line as they were introduced to each member of staff. When the introductions were complete and they all knew their respective rooms, the children were eager to explore more of their new surroundings.

'Can we go out for a look around the farm now?' asked Wilfred.

'Mind the dogs; some of them bite. They're not as friendly as at home. Best to stay away from them until they get used to you,' warned Henry.

'All right, Father,' said Wilfred, dashing like a madman round to the rear buildings. Some of the barns had sheep and lambs in them. They bleated pitifully when they saw the faces of the children.

There was quite a din coming from the hut the men slept in. They had finished their tucker and were enjoying a few beers. It seemed the Australians had always loved their beer. Already they were starting to sing country songs passed down by the early settlers.

'Father said we mustn't go in that hut. It's for adults only,' said Victoria.

As the lights went down and darkness invaded the farm the children were fascinated, listening to the Aborigines blowing their horns. That deep, throbbing note, so at home in the outback of Australia. When the children went to bed that night it was the throbbing of the pipes that lulled them to sleep.

The next day, after a hearty breakfast of steak and fried eggs, the children went for a buggy ride and in the afternoon were given their first lessons in how to ride a horse. The children loved horse riding and within a few days could mount and dismount unaided, and canter and gallop across the green pastures.

However, it couldn't be all play and no work. There was no school for a hundred miles, so the job of teaching fell on Mary's shoulders. Besides, it gave her something to do. She made sure the children all kept up their studies. This worked out fine as the three children were keen pupils. Unfortunately, Rose was years behind the others, but she made steady progress and soon she would master reading and writing.

Mary began to learn, at her own insistence, how to handle the sheep. She already knew a lot from the days spent on her father's estate. The work on this farm was so different to back on her father's farm twenty-five years ago. It was much harder here, but she enjoyed it, and was prepared to work with the farmhands late into the night when the lambing season started.

A couple of days after their arrival, there was the sound of running feet on the veranda and an Aborigine, whom they had nicknamed Mikano, came to the door, very excited. Wilfred and Victoria, and indeed Mary, had never seen an Aborigine before coming to the farm, let alone spoken to one. He was so like the pictures one had seen in the books, very brown, with frizzy, unkempt hair and flared nostrils. Not many Aborigines spoke English. It was only because of a missionary school, which had opened up for a year before disbanding, that some of the children had learnt English.

This young man had shown an interest in the farm, so Henry had taken him on. Mikano was so good with the animals that Henry had come to respect him and his views. He wore a chequered shirt and ragged brown trousers, but his head and feet were bare.

'Boss, come quick, some them sheep really sick, they can't stand up, two sheep have died,' rambled Mikano, who was acting as Henry's head shepherd.

Henry was very alarmed at this news. He had been lucky for a number of years because he had had no serious diseases in his flocks. Some of his neighbours had not been so fortunate and had lost everything. He ran after Mikano, who was leading him to where the sick sheep were. He recognised the terribly infectious condition within a few moments of their arrival.

'It's scabies,' Henry said resignedly. This was one of the worse things that could happen to a sheep farmer. 'Right, Mikano, you must not let anybody come on the farm. If people want to come they must wash their shoes and boots first.'

Mikano looked at Henry, bewildered. 'What you mean, boss? They have to wash all over?'

'No, just the boots they walk in, that's all.'

'Why, boss?'

'Because they bring this disease from another farm. We must stop it spreading. We have to keep these sheep away from the good ones. Then we wash them with coal tar to help kill the disease. You understand, Mikano?'

'Yes, yes, boss, I think so.' He looked at Henry and repeated his instructions to make sure he had got them right. 'So if you go off the farm you must wash boots when you come back?'

'That's right, you've got it.'

They set about sorting out the sheep that appeared sick from the fit ones, but found the number infected was growing and growing.

'What we gonna do, boss?'

'I don't know the answer. These sick sheep won't get better. Round them all up, drive them away off the farm and we will shoot them all. Don't let them get on grass used for grazing. Get the boys to help and be quick. Make sure you take every one, no matter how many. Get going.'

Henry went to get the rifles. His mind was in a state of panic. Up to now he had always managed to avoid getting this terrible disease on his farm. Some of his friends had lost everything when this plague had struck their farms. He was determined to take all preventive measures to save as much of his flock as possible.

As soon as he entered the house Wilfred looked up from the history book he was studying. He could see the look of anguish on his father's face and knew something was wrong.

'What's the trouble, Father?'

'Half the flock are sick. If we are not careful we will have none left. Come on, Wilfred, I need your help. We have to shoot the sick sheep.'

Wilfred, who was against killing animals of any kind, realised right away that this was a life-or-death predicament and it was no time to stand on silly, outdated values. The livelihood of the family was at stake. He dropped his book and took the rifle his father gave him. They grabbed their horses and raced after the sheep, taking care not to scatter them.

'This will do, Mikano. Pen them in, otherwise they will run when we start shooting.'

All the men were lending a hand. By working as a team they managed to get the sick animals isolated. Having ensured the pens were secure, Henry gave the order to start shooting the sheep. It was not a pretty sight. How he wished there was an alternative to shooting them, but he couldn't risk infecting the remainder of his sheep. Tomorrow they would have to visit all their flocks and kill off any that were sick.

They were doing so much shooting that the guns were getting too hot to handle. The dead sheep were piling high and the noise was deafening, from the sheep and from the farmhands.

'OK, that's enough for tonight,' called Henry, signalling for the men to stop shooting and secure the pens for the night.

Suddenly a big infected ram jumped up on the back of another and leapt out of the pen. It started running towards the animals that weren't sick. Wilfred was about to chase after the ram.

'Leave it, Wilfred, I will get it,' shouted Henry, and with that he chased after it. His horse didn't see the rabbit hole and stuck its hoof in it, throwing Henry onto his head. He lay there unconscious. All who saw the accident ran to where Henry lay.

'Get Mother, quick,' shouted Wilfred to Mikano.

Mikano jumped on his horse and sped across the grasslands to the house. He leapt off his horse before it had come to a halt.

'Miss Mary, come quick, the master boss has fallen off his horse. He hurt badly. Come quick.'

'Oh, no, not again,' she said as she removed her pinafore and jumped up behind Mikano.

'Hold tight. I in a big hurry,' he said, galloping off.

Mary jumped off the horse and ran to her husband's side. He was still unconscious.

'Get the wagon, and get him back to the house quickly,' she ordered those around her. Henry was gently lifted onto the wagon.

At the house many willing hands offered to take Henry inside.

'Handle him gently,' commanded Mary. 'Lay him on the couch. Wilfred, go and fetch a doctor.' There was a doctor's practice about five miles away. In fact a small village commune had started there; it was nice to have neighbours who weren't a hundred miles away.

Mary sent all the workers away for the night, and attended to her poor husband. She bathed his head in cold water and checked over his body to see if there were any broken bones. It looked as if her bad luck with men was still with her. She had already lost the best five men in her life, and didn't want to add Henry to the list.

'Oh, my head,' said Henry as he came to. 'Mary, I can't see. It's like it used to be when I was caught in the fire in that hotel in London. I can't see. That blow on the head has brought back my loss of sight.'

'Don't despair, my darling; things have improved immensely since then. It is surprising what the doctors can do today. You just lie still; the doctor will be here soon.'

Henry lay back and closed his eyes, even though it was constant blackness.

They heard the doctor stomping on the veranda as he arrived. Johnny Meadows was the only doctor for miles in any direction. It took a day for him just to get to some patients. Fortunately for Henry, the doctor's house was in the next shanty town, which had grown up since Henry had first come here seven years ago.

Johnny, like most men in the area, didn't dress for the occasion. He wore a large slouch hat, shirt and trousers – nothing fancy. He drove a horse and two-wheeled rig in which was his black bag. The doctor was a happily married man with twin three-year-old girls, and a pretty wife called April. She was thirty that day.

'Well, Henry, what have you been up to this time?' he asked cheerily.

'Hi, doc! I have lost my eyesight again.'

'You mean you lost it before?'

'Yes, about seven years ago in London. Funnily enough it was a fall from a horse which brought it back then.'

'Let's have a look,' the doctor said, rummaging in his bag. 'Open your eyes wide.' He struck a match. 'Can you see this light, Henry?'

'I can see a glimmer, but that's all.'

'Well, there's nothing I can do. I suggest we leave it for a while. Give the eyes a rest; they may come back to full vision of their own accord. I don't think any serious, long-term damage has been done,' he said, fastening his bag and standing up. 'Just rest. If the sight should return, let me know. I will come out and see you in a week's time.'

'Fine. Thanks, doc,' said Henry, with a smile.

Once everyone had gone and they were the only two left, Mary went to the settee and, sitting down, took Henry's hand. 'Don't worry, my love. Remember when you lost your sight last time I promised you I would be your eyes, and I will once again.'

'Thank you, Mary. I feel so helpless, especially now we have the flock down with this disease.'

'The last thing you need now is worry, and anyway there is nothing you can do till morning, so just relax,' she said firmly.

The next morning, Mikano and the other hands, together with Mary and Wilfred, resumed the shooting of the sick sheep and inspecting the rest of their huge flock. It was lucky for them that the disease was contained and had not spread. They had caught it just in time, though this did not mean they could become complacent. Henry just could not relax; he wanted to know everything that was going on.

Mary was so pleased to be with her stepbrother again. 'Do you ever hear from your sister? She lives in Australia, doesn't she, Alex?' she asked him, a week after the accident.

'I think she does. She left our home in Newcastle in England... let me see... it would be fourteen years ago. I was away from home then. I have never seen her since.'

'She's my stepsister too, you know,' said Mary.

'Of course she is; I forgot,' said Alex, putting his arm round Mary. He had really taken to her; she was so sensible and efficient.

'I think I'll write to John and find out where she is living,' said Mary.

The doctor came that evening to see how Henry was. He gave Henry another good check-over.

'I'm afraid there's nothing for it, old chap. You won't get your eyesight back unless you return to England, where they now have much better resources than we do, and are years ahead at fixing eyes. If you want to see again then you must go to England. I will write the report and I know a first-class Harley Street specialist who will perform the operation. Are you game?'

'Have I got a choice? I have just arrived back from England.'

'Not if you want to see again.'

'Thank you, doctor. I must first discuss it with my wife. Can I let you know tomorrow?'

'There's no need for that, doctor. We will go to England. Please make your arrangements,' said Mary, firmly. Henry knew it was pointless to argue with her.

After the doctor had left, Mary called all the family together to discuss the matter. She had obviously already made her mind up as to how it was to be done.

'Right, family, and that means all of you, we need to make some decisions regarding your father's health. If we can get him to England there is a good chance he will get his sight back, but we can't all go. So this is what I propose. Henry and I will go to England. Wilfred, you will stay in charge here, together with your uncle Alex and sister. Rose is not well enough to travel. However, I am hopeful of getting the correct medicine for her while I am in England, so that she can be cured.'

'It will mean, Wilfred, you will have to run the farm. You have two superb advisors in Alex and Mikano. Can I rely on you to take over for a period of approximately six months?' asked Henry.

'Of course you can, Father,' Wilfred replied instantly. Henry was proud of his son, who was only fourteen.

'Right, that's settled. I will arrange the tickets. I know our parents will be delighted to see us, and I think it will be the last time we see them alive as they are getting very old and infirm,' said Mary.

'Try and see our father, Mary' said Alex, anxiously.

'Of course I will. I know he will be delighted to see Henry again. He always said he would make a wonderful husband for me, and he was right,' said Mary, squeezing Henry's hand in affection.

'Right, all back to work,' said Wilfred, taking up the reins of authority.

Mary was very distraught when she was told by the authorities of the *Great Britain* that the captain of the ship was missing and the *Great Britain* wouldn't sail until he was found.

'How long will that be?' she asked.

'At least two weeks, madam. I'm sorry I can't be of more help,' said the second officer.

Mary returned to the farm to tell Henry the news. 'We can't go back to England for at least two weeks, my love.'

'Why? What's the hold-up?' Henry asked. Mary told him of John's disappearance. He was shocked.

'How are the sheep? Have we got rid of that disease?'

'Yes. As far as we can tell, the flock is now cured.'

'How many dead ones have we?'

'Three hundred and thirty. We have 1,700 healthy sheep. So you can stop worrying, dearest,' said Mary, adjusting his pillows.

'I do wish I could be out there seeing what's going on,' said Henry.

'Well, you can't. Wilfred is doing a grand job along with the ranch hands. You should be proud of him.'

'Yes, I am,' he sighed.

Rose hadn't improved a great deal, and she hadn't got worse. It was becoming like a hospital, thought Mary. It was a good job she had her nursing training for her life in Australia.

So life went on, pretty much the same.

Alex returned to prison. The reason why he had to do this was because the last time he had been in England, some fifteen years ago, he had been a vagrant, with no money. One night he had tried to rob Henry and Mary at gunpoint while they were on a night out in London. Henry disarmed him and handed him over to the police. It was only when they went to court for his trial that Mary saw her real father once more. She was surprised to see him at the Old Bailey, until he pointed out that the man being charged with robbery was actually her brother. They had never met, and didn't know each other. His name was Alex, she was told.

At the trial Alex was convicted of attempted robbery and sentenced to prison in Australia. When the court closed Mary felt very sad at seeing her father crying at the sentence imposed on his son. Henry suddenly came up with an idea, and went to see the clerk of the court. He explained that he had a sheep farm in Australia and would be happy to employ Alex on his farm and to see to his security. This was most unusual. The judge, having heard the offer, said he would allow this to happen on condition that Alex had to do five years of his sentence before he could be released on parole. Every six months he would also have to report back to the jail, where he would stay for a week before being sent back to the farm. This was far better than ever Alex, his father or sister could have imagined and they were all very grateful to Henry for his kind offer. That was how Alex had now become foreman on the farm. However, he still wasn't a free man, and had to go back to prison every six months.

Alex had taken to his young nephew, despite the fact that Wilfred had an air of snobbery about him; they got on very well and the young man was quickly learning all about sheep farming. As Alex was doing his week in prison at the moment, however, it was Mikano who now took Wilfred up into the hills to see the flock's condition and do a head count.

'See there is no water coming, Master Wilfred,' said Mikano.

They both surveyed the scene around them, and indeed the grass was short and very dry.

'Rain not come for another two months. Lucky we have river.'

'Yes, but I see the level is down by half,' said Wilfred. 'We will just have to be careful with it. Come on, Mikano, let's get back to the ranch.' He cantered off.

When Wilfred got back to the farm, he gave the reins of his horse to a farmhand. He walked up the stairs into the house; it was quiet. He heard coughing in Rose's bedroom and gently tapped on the door. Mary was tending Rose, who was having a coughing fit.

'Still no sign of her getting better?' he observed.

'No. I fear it is consumption as she is spitting out blood now. Oh, if only we were back in England.' Mary had seen so many cases of this disease in her lifetime of nursing. She knew there was no cure. Perhaps there was some new medication she knew nothing about.

'Why don't you take her back to England with you?' suggested Wilfred.

'That's a good idea, my son. We can get her the best treatment home in London. I will speak to your father and see what he says; I'm sure he will agree,' said Mary.

They sat down for lunch. It was a beautiful warm sunny day, like every day seemed to be in Australia.

Wilfred looked out of the window. 'That's a dark cloud over there. Do you think we are going to have some rain? We could certainly do with it.'

Henry raised his head. 'I can't see anything, but I can smell burning. I think the grass is on fire,' he said.

'Oh no. Will it spread, Father?' asked Wilfred, running outside. Now he could plainly see it was a huge cloud of smoke, a grassland fire, and by the drift of the smoke cloud it was headed in their direction. He would have to do whatever he could to protect the flock.

'What shall we do, Father?' asked Wilfred. This was a possible catastrophe he was not familiar with.

'We need to get all the sheep on the other side of the river bank, son; that way we will hopefully have a fire break.'

'What about the house, Father?'

'That, my son, is in the lap of God. Hopefully it won't come this far. Get going, move the sheep, that's your priority.'

'Yes, Father.' He ran to find Mikano. 'Start moving the sheep to the other side of the river,' he instructed him, trying not to show he was in a panic.

Mikano went and got all the sheep herders out, and the dogs. He told the men what they had to do. They could see for themselves how big the fire was getting and rallied round, giving full support to the problem. By late afternoon all the sheep were on the far river bank.

'I don't think there is any more we can do,' said Wilfred.

'No,' said Mikano, 'but if the wind changes we must get sheep back.'

That night the sky was lit by the fire burning just a few miles away. Black smoke could be smelt on the farm, and some were already coughing.

'I do hope it doesn't come this far. We could lose everything,' said Mary.

'Are there any firefighters, like we have in London, Father?'

'Just a handful of volunteers, son. They are not trained, nor do they have the facilities for big fires like this. We just have to let it burn itself out, which could take days, even weeks.'

They all felt so helpless.

'Alex is due out of prison today,' said Henry. 'Will you arrange for Mikano to take the buggy and pick him up at the quay, son? We need Alex here now we have a new crisis.'

Wilfred passed the order on to Mikano.

'Don't worry, boss, I fix it,' Mikano said, with his usual happy smile.

Mikano drove to the town well aware the fire was heading in his direction. Hundreds of people were out with branches from the trees, trying to stop the fire spreading.

'Can I get into town?' he asked a farmer.

'Just about. Be careful; the fire is spreading everywhere.'

Mikano drove on. He put a wet handkerchief over his face and made a detour round the fire. He managed to get into town, and to the docks. Alex was sitting on a pile of boxes, waiting for him. The black smoke had already darkened the sky but luckily the fire had not come this far.

'Mikano, am I glad to see you! Thank you for coming.'

'It is fine, no problem. Well, only the fire. It is growing fast. Master boss is worried about the farm.'

'What about the sheep?' asked Alex.

'Sheep all right. We move to other river bank. Men staying to look after them.'

'That's good,' said Alex. 'Can we get to the ranch, Mikano?'

'Yes, we will try,' he said, cracking his whip.

They rode for some ten miles.

'Wind change way it blows,' said Mikano. 'Not good for us but OK for farm.'

'We should be all right, shouldn't we?' asked Alex, trying hard to work out the direction it was to the ranch, because Mikano had to keep well to the left. They were a mile from the well-worn track they usually used when going to town.

'I think we should stop at the next building built of stone and ask for protection from the fire till it's past.'

'Not a wooden one?' asked Alex.

'No, Alex, just stone, no burn,' said Mikano.

'OK, there is one ahead; we will call in there. We can't go any further. The smoke is choking and blinding me,' said Alex.

'This good, old stone building. Nobody live there for long time. Now a pigsty,' said Mikano.

'How do you know, Mikano?'

'I know old man who live there before. Now it is a pigsty, dirty and smelly.'

'It will do us till tomorrow, till the fire is past.'

'OK! We call.'

Alex banged on the door. No answer.

'You sure nobody lives here?'

'Sure, me positive. Sometimes I see man go in or come out. No misses or kids. Just empty house, falling down.'

Still no reply.

'I hear a voice,' said Alex. 'Hello! Anyone in there?' he shouted.

There was a muffled reply from inside the house. Alex couldn't make out what was said, but at least he knew the house was occupied.

'I don't know what to do, but there is someone in there, Mikano.'

Suddenly a window high up the wall was smashed and a shoe landed on the ground.

'Something is wrong. Help me break the door down.'

They both pushed and the door gave way.

'Christ! You were right when you said it was a pigsty, yet someone is living here. Must be a shortage of houses. Try this door.'

It opened into a near-dark room. They saw a man lying on a bed.

'Hello,' said Alex. 'Sorry about breaking in. We thought you had a problem when the window smashed and a shoe fell out.'

'I am Captain John Gray of the *Great Britain* ocean liner and I have been kidnapped, fed only bread and water and chained up with no exercise for a fortnight. Who are you? Have you come to rescue me?'

'Who did this to you?'

'I don't know. There are keys to the handcuffs hanging on that door over there.'

Alex was about to go for the keys when another man appeared through the door.

'What are you two doing in my house?' demanded the man, who was wearing a mask to hide his face.

Mikano made a move towards the door, muttering as he went. 'I go put horse and buggy in the barn next door, keep safe from fire.'

'Stay where you are, if you value your life. I have a gun here. I own this house and this man on the bed is my prisoner. You are intruders; get out of my house!' the masked man shouted.

'What do you mean? You can't just chain people up. You could be hanged for that,' said Alex.

'I go get policeman,' said Mikano, making a dash for the open door. The man turned and fired a shot after him. Alex kicked the door shut on the man's arm; he howled and dropped the pistol. Alex got him in a half-nelson grip which immobilised him. He reached for the handcuff keys and threw it to John to free himself, which he quickly accomplished.

'Go and see to Mikano,' Alex said.

John went to find the Aborigine.

'Your friend is dead,' said John.

Alex was sad and shocked when told this. Mikano had been a good, reliable friend. 'You will hang for this, you bastard,' said Alex to the masked man.

'What, for killing an Abo? You're mistaken, my friend. I will probably get a medal,' he scoffed.

'You're no friend of mine, you murderer. John, get the keys and put the chains on him.' When that was completed, they searched the man and removed his false mask and beard.

'I know who this is,' said John. 'It's Toby Dowdy, the man I locked up when he was a passenger on the *Great Britain*. I recognise him as he has only one eye.'

'Why did you lock him up?' asked Alex.

'He socked me on the jaw and knocked me to the ground when I was trying to resolve some differences between the steerage passengers and the galley who prepared the food. So I put him in irons on bread and water, and he has retaliated by doing the same to me. Only he got greedy and demanded a ransom of £500 for my release.'

'That's enough to hang him, without the murder of my friend,' said Alex.

'What shall we do now?' asked John. 'I must get back to my ship.'

'There is a raging inferno going on outside, covering acres of grassland. We just happened on this stone-built house to stay in until it had passed. That is how we came to find and release you. We must stay here till morning. I'm sorry; it's too dangerous to do otherwise.' Alex looked around. 'Is there any food?'

'There may be some bread and water that this tyke brought for my next meal. You and I can share it.'

'Come on, let's have a look at Mikano.'

He was lying face-down. They turned him over; the bullet had entered his heart through his back.

They closed his eyes and covered him with the blanket they ripped off the bed.

'Indirectly, he saved our lives,' said Alex.

'I know,' said John. 'He knew the risk he was taking. I'm sure he will be sadly missed by those who knew him.'

'He was a good workman and friend,' said Alex.

'It's getting hot in here,' said John.

'Don't worry, it will soon pass. I have experienced these fires before. We should be safe enough here till morning,' said Alex.

Next morning, after a very hard and uncomfortable night, they uncuffed their captive and got the horse and buggy out of the stable. As they had no rope or handcuffs to keep him secure, Toby Dowdy decided to make a break for it.

'Stop! Or I fire,' shouted Alex. The man ignored him and ran towards the flames. Alex fired twice; both shots hit Dowdy in the back. He fell down, and didn't move again.

'That will save the county a great deal of money,' said Alex, as he threw the pistol into the raging fire.

'Shouldn't we see if he is dead?' asked John, looking very concerned.

'No, he's dead all right. We will leave him where he lies. It can be his cremation spot. The fire is heading this way.'

'I want to get back to my ship,' said John.

'Not today, sonny boy,' said Alex. 'We are cut off from the city. We have two choices. Either we stay here and die because we have no food or water, and are surrounded by the fire, or we make a dash for the ranch, which is only fifteen miles away.'

John reluctantly chose the latter option.

Meanwhile, back at the ranch, there was great concern as to what had happened to the two men.

'They should be back here by now,' said Henry.

'Don't worry, my love, they're not babies and can think for themselves. They won't risk the fire hazard. They'll have found a safe hiding until tomorrow; you can be sure of that,' said Mary, staring out the window in the direction of town.

'They're here, they're here, Mother, I can see them racing towards us,' shouted Victoria, excitedly.

The family gathered at the window.

'Who is the stranger?' asked Wilfred.

'And where is Mikano?' asked Mary.

The buggy stopped outside the door, and the two men alighted and went into the house.

'Hello. What a journey we have had,' said Alex. He pointed to John. 'I expect you recognise my companion.'

'Yes, it's the captain of the *Great Britain*. John Gray, isn't it?'

'That's right, madam, and you are, I believe, Mary Harper, and this is your husband Henry.'

'Yes. Henry has gone blind again.'

'Alex was explaining it all to me. I believe you're coming back on my ship.'

'Yes, Captain. How long do you think before you leave for England?'

'Well, I want to get back for Christmas, so I would think two weeks' time would be the limit.'

'We're starving, little sister. What an adventure we had.'

They sat down and within ten minutes they had a cooked breakfast of lamb steaks and eggs, followed by lots of hot coffee. Alex and John related their story to the family as they were eating.

'So poor Mikano is dead. He was a good man and will be sorely missed. We have had a telegram to say that the city and port are cut off. The wind is blowing the flames into the town. The *Great Britain* has left its mooring and gone off shore to deeper water until the fire has burnt out,' said Henry.

'Good, that makes good sense,' said John, wiping his plate clean with a hunk of bread. He leaned back in his chair. 'My, it's fine to be out of the stink hole I was imprisoned in.'

'Yes, you were lucky Mikano knew of the old stone house, otherwise we might never have known what had happened to you,' said Henry. 'What a horrid, vindictive man your jailor must have been.'

'What can I do to help out, here at the sheep farm?' asked John.

'You are our guest, John; relax and enjoy yourself. Can you ride a horse?'

'I have done years ago.'

'Good, we will get you back in the saddle; would you like that? It means you can look over the farm,' said Mary.

'Yes, that would be fine,' he said, with a cheery smile.

'Would you like to send a telegram to your ship to tell them not to worry and that you are well and safe?' asked Henry.

'Could I do that? I would be very relieved to be able to do so,' said John.

'Well, we might be lucky, if there's no fire damage. Wilfred will do it for us, won't you, son?'

'Right away, Father,' he responded. 'Come with me, Captain, and we will see what we can do.'

After five attempts they were able to get a message through to the ss *Great Britain*.

Three days later, the family received notification that the fire had been extinguished, and, apart from smoke, normal life could resume. Although

John had enjoyed himself at the farm, he couldn't wait to get back to his ship. Alex drove him into town and to where the ship had re-berthed. They parted as lifelong friends, both of them remembering so well the happenings at the old stone pigsty.

CHAPTER 8

Alex had been recalled to prison but he didn't understand why, as he had not been long away. Word had reached the prison authorities about how he had saved the life of Captain Gray. They explained that Alex had proved himself to be a reliable, hard-working man, and they had decided to release him and give him his freedom. For saving the captain's life he was awarded 1,000 acres of grassland and £100. Alex was shocked and delighted. There was a picture of him in the city newspaper and a write-up on his bravery, plus his freedom and award. He sang all the way back to the farm. He was very happy because he had proved he could hold down a job and be an asset to Australia. The prison committee had decided not only to make him a free man but to allow him to become a fully-fledged Australian.

Henry was delighted for him, as was Mary. However, they didn't want to lose him and made it plain that there was always a home with them.

Alex was fifty-five years old but looked nearer seventy; the hard work on the farm, and prison life and food, had all helped to age him. But he was strong and wiry and had many years of useful work in him.

It was a fine day and Alex wanted to develop some ground at the back of the farm. It meant pulling down some sheds and sowing the ground with grass seed. He used four other men to pull the old sheds down. It was hot, thirsty work. Alex was not a man to sit back and let the others do it all, so as well as directing operations he got stuck in with the others. As the sheds were pulled down, the timber was stacked in piles depending on its condition. It was dirty, dusty work, but the men got stuck in, joking with each other and laughing as they went about their labour.

Alex was unscrewing a hinge that was old and rusty. He was not a man to give in, and in trying to dislodge it, he dropped the screwdriver, which rolled under the floor of the shed. He could see part of the handle, so he bent to pick it up. As he did so his hand received a sharp bite from a funnel-web spider that was heavy with eggs.

'Christ!' shouted Alex, as he stepped back in alarm. He knew what had happened, and knew that his chance of recovery would dwindle in minutes without immediate and drastic medical attention.

'What's up, Alex?' shouted Tim, the new foreman.

'A funnel spider has just bitten me,' replied Alex, sucking the poison from his finger and spitting it out onto the ground.

Tim never wasted a moment; he dashed over to where Alex stood nursing his finger and drew a huge knife from his belt. He grabbed Alex's hand, laid it on a plank of wood and with one almighty swipe chopped off the finger that had been bitten.

'Thanks, mate, but that was a bit drastic, cutting my bloody finger off,' said Alex, trying to stop the blood flow with his shirt. 'Still, I guess you may have saved my life, sport.'

'There is no cure for that bite. Good job it was your finger, not your leg, otherwise you'd be dead soon,' said Tim. 'Maybe we are in time and have caught the poison before it could run into your whole body. Go and lie down, Alex; you are not fit for work today.'

Alex took his advice and went to the big house. Mary was writing a letter when she saw him stagger into the entrance hall, clutching his hand, which had been wrapped in a neck bandana to stop the blood.

'What's the matter? Have you had an accident?' asked Mary, leaving what she was doing and getting up to see to her brother. She could see he was in pain and it took a couple of moments before she realised that his middle finger was missing. Blood was squirting everywhere; not that Mary minded the mess. She was more concerned for her brother, who was very ill.

'Oh, my dear boy, what's happened to your finger? Come and lie on the settee. I will dress your hand. I wish Wilfred were here, but he's up on the top meadow. I will wake Henry up, and see if he can advise.'

When Henry was awakened he was very concerned at the news of what had happened to Alex.

'Get the doctor quickly. This is very serious,' said Henry.

Alex's face had gone bright red. Mary took all situations like this very coolly. She had seen the worst inhumanities imaginable done to the human body when serving in Crimea. Death had been as common as the atrocious weather they had to endure.

'Water, I need water, quick,' cried out Alex. Mary went and fetched him a glass, which he emptied right away.

'Christ, it hurts like hell,' said Alex. 'I've been bitten by a spider and Tim has cut my finger off. It bloody hurts like hell.'

'What was it, a funnel-web?' she asked, very concerned. She knew all about these terrifying creatures and their lethal bite. There was no cure, only the immediate amputation of the limb concerned to stop the poison spreading. If this wasn't done in time then normally it resulted in a funeral.

Alex started to doze off.

'Stay awake, Alex. How do you feel?'

'Bloody groggy.' He lay back, resting his hand on his lap and his head on the backrest of the chair.

Tim came to the porch and knocked on the door. Mary looked up and, seeing who it was, asked him in.

'Alex, how are you? Have you sent for the doctor yet?' asked Tim.

'Yes, we have; he's out on call. We have left an emergency call,' said Mary.

Alex had fallen unconscious again. She bathed his brow. There was nothing she could do now but wait for the doctor. She hoped he would make a recovery, but she had her doubts. There wasn't a hospital within

200 miles. There was nothing more she could do but pray for Alex and hope that Tim's speedy response in cutting off his finger had been in time to stop the poison circulating in his bloodstream.

As the family came in for midday food they all looked at Alex and enquired what was wrong with him. No one in or near the family had been bitten like this before; it was very rare, and very unfortunate. Alex was sweating; his clothes were saturated. He was hot and running a temperature. The hand had become very swollen.

'What's the matter with Alex?' asked Wilfred, as he clumped into the lounge.

'He's been bitten by a funnel-web.'

'Has he? Oh, Christ! There's not much hope for him then, poor devil. Is the doctor coming?'

'He should be here soon. Oh, I do hope he recovers. Tim cut his finger off to try and save his life.' Mary looked at her brother, wondering what more they could do.

'It's in the lap of the gods, my dear,' said Henry. 'We must wait and see what tomorrow brings.'

'I will sleep in a chair by his side tonight in case he needs help,' said Mary, as she tucked the blanket round him.

'It's at times like this I wish we had a hospital nearer,' said Henry.

There was a knock at the door; it was the doctor.

'It's Alex, doctor. He has been bitten by a funnel,' said Mary.

'You're certainly getting your share of bad luck.'

'More than our share,' said Henry.

Alex was now in a coma. His mind kept drifting back to his youth. He remembered his hours spent as a cabin boy on the *Tipperary* whaling ship. He remembered the crew and the big seas the whaler fished on. He had stuck it for two years before joining the Queen's navy. He was a powder monkey, running backwards and forwards getting powder for the guns and water for the crew.

He liked that life, but then one day he got clipped by a musket ball on his right shoulder and the navy wouldn't let him serve any more. He tried many jobs but couldn't settle. Then he took to drink. He lived with the winos and down-and-outs in Waterloo. He couldn't get enough money to satisfy his thirst, and that was when he took to robbing people in the dark streets at night. It was on one such occasion he tried to hold up Henry and Mary, not knowing Mary was his stepsister. Henry disarmed him and handed him over to the constable. As a result of that robbery he was sent to a prison in Australia. He realised his life had, in the main, been wasted.

In the distance he was aware of voices; he could just make out the doctor's voice.

'I fear the poison is in his system. It attacks the nervous system, and the funnel and redback spiders are ones to be avoided. One day, hopefully, we will have a medicine to cure these bites, but I have never seen anyone recover yet,' the doctor said, shaking his head. 'Here is some aspirin. Give him one every three hours. No more, do you understand?'

'Yes, doctor, thank you,' said Mary.

The doctor shook his head in recognition that there was nothing more he could do. He felt so helpless, so ineffectual. 'Give me a call if he should get worse or die,' he said, as he left the house.

Alex heard this; he knew only too well what the final outcome would be. He just wished the throbbing pain of his missing finger would subside.

Mary sat by his bed on the settee that night. It was very uncomfortable in the chair, but she couldn't leave him. She bathed and freshly dressed his wounded hand, which had puffed up to twice its size. She looked at it, and felt there should be something she could do. What would she have done in Crimea? she asked herself. Would she have taken a chance on home surgery, if she thought it might relieve pain and suffering?

She coaxed another aspirin into his mouth with a sip of water. He opened his eyes and smiled at her. 'Thanks,' was all he managed to whisper.

Mary checked the time: it was two o'clock, not that it mattered. Alex had gone back to sleep. Henry could be heard snoring loudly from their bedroom at the back of the house. The other members of the family were all asleep. She bathed Alex's sweaty hot forehead once more. She felt it was decision time.

Leaving the room, she went into the kitchen and found the sharpest knife she had. She took a clean tablecloth from the drawer and started tearing it into strips for bandages.

Next, she sharpened the knife to get a really keen edge on it. She wanted to make sure the knife was clear of infection, so she went over to the dying kitchen range fire and plunged the blade into the hot embers until she was satisfied it was ready.

She drew her chair up close to the settee. She placed the oil lamp so that it illuminated the area she planned to work on. She tried to remember what she used to do to the poor wounded and dying soldiers in Crimea. She decided she ought to wake Alex up and tell him what she intended to do. She rocked him gently.

'Alex, Alex, can you hear me?'

Eventually, he managed to open his eyes. 'Yes.'

'I'm going to cut your hand to release the poison; it will hurt. Be brave, little brother; it is the only hope I have of saving your life.'

'Go ahead,' he said, falling back to sleep.

She took his swollen hand in hers, and placed it on a clean cloth. Mary had a good knowledge of the make-up of the human body; where the main muscles and arteries were. Using this knowledge, she made the incision where she thought the greatest pressure of poison was. She probed a little further down into the hand. Suddenly there was a fountain of blood and pus shooting from the hand. She knew she daren't stop now. She squeezed the hand until nothing more came out of it. The cut was only small, so it wouldn't need a stitch. She bathed the wound, and already a more natural colour was returning to the hand. She decided to put a stitch into the finger that had been amputated. Alex didn't stir, but a better colour was coming to his face.

As Mary went to fetch clean bandages, she suddenly remembered something she had brought from England. Amongst many other medications she had purchased was a good-quality healing cream. Mary applied a generous quantity of the cream to a pad, and pressed it firmly down on the incision. She wrapped the hand, and replaced it in a sling round Alex's neck. Satisfied she had done all she could, she cleared up the mess and fell asleep in the chair, exhausted.

In the morning when Henry came in, Alex was still in a coma, and Mary had stayed by his bedside all night. He was still running a high temperature and nothing they could do would shift it. The hand she had operated on was much better, but there was no guarantee that the poison hadn't already spread into his body. There was no point calling the doctor out again; he could do nothing more.

'Come away, Mary, he is sleeping. You go and get some sleep yourself,' said Henry. He didn't expect miracles. Alex had not only been bitten by one of the world's most poisonous spiders, but he had lost a lot of blood where he had had his finger chopped off by Tim.

By midday Alex was still asleep. Mary felt his pulse; it was very irregular. She opened his shirt and put her hand on his heart; again the beats were irregular and slow.

Tim came to the door; he had brought the local medicine man, an Aborigine, with him. 'Mr Henry, this is a good medicine man; he has cured spider bites before, he said. Do you want him to heal Alex?'

Henry shook his head. 'It's too late for that. I fear it is only a matter of time. Thank you, Tim, but tell your man we don't want his services.'

The two men left, mumbling together.

At three in the afternoon, Alex gave a cough and passed away. Mary went and felt for a pulse, but there was none. She straightened with tears running down her face she drew the blanket over Alex's face and body.

'He's passed away, Henry. He never recovered.'

Mary was very upset; after all, even though he was only her stepbrother, she had grown to love and respect him as if he had been her own flesh and blood. She raised a cloth to her eyes to cover the tears. Even though she had seen so much death in her life, the loss of Alex, whom she had grown to love, hurt her greatly.

As John climbed up the gangplank to his ship, all the crew were gathered to greet him. Many had thought he was dead. John shook hands with all of them. He was particularly pleased to see his first and second officers. 'Thank you both for looking after my ship,' he said.

He looked around the top deck. The ship looked ready for sea. He saw that the wooden deck had been scrubbed and caulked. The sails were all in position. He wanted to inspect below but waited till he could have a conference with his officers.

'Come to my cabin and we will discuss the date of departure,' he said. 'My instructions say we have to depart no later than the twenty-second of October. If we do then we should be home for Christmas.'

The two senior officers were like two happy boys, and couldn't wait to find out what had happened to their captain. 'It's good to see you back, Captain. When we received the ransom demand we feared the worst.'

John made light of what had happened. 'Yes, it wasn't very pleasant being chained up and fed on bread and water.'

'What? They actually did this to you, sir?'

He nodded. 'I was freed by two men a fortnight later, and the perpetrator was shot dead.'

'Good show,' said the first officer. 'No more than he deserved. Who was it, sir?'

'I'd rather not say. Let's forget the whole episode and talk about the ship and her return to England,' said John.

'Are we going through the Suez again, sir?'

'We certainly are not,' he responded, emphatically. His officers smiled at each other, because up till that moment they hadn't been sure. They could understand their captain's reluctance to try the Suez again. The canal itself was fine. It was the people who lived along it that caused the complications.

'When shall we start taking passengers on board, sir?' asked the first officer.

'Are we fully provisioned?' asked John.

'No, sir, not yet. We have some animals and birds left, which we saved by taking the shorter route through the Suez. I am expecting the replacement farm animals next Wednesday. We have coal and water for the return journey.'

'How many passengers have we?'

'Only 125 so far, Captain. We are expecting another fifty. We are thirty men short on our crew register.'

'Why's that?'

'They have deserted the ship in favour of gold mining.'

'It always happens this way,' said John. 'See if you can recruit more people. I only want good workers.'

Chapter 9

Although it was early in the morning, the local sheriff Jeff Frisby was awake. He had heard the shot in the night and guessed someone had been shot. He peered out of his bedroom window and saw two men escorting three others at gunpoint towards his little jailhouse. It wasn't often he had guests in his jail; when he did, he would have to wait till the circuit judge came to the town. The judge was due in four days' time. He would hear the charges and hold court, and then pronounce the punishment.

Jeff ran downstairs and lit the oil lamp. There was a knock on the jailhouse door. He opened it.

'Bloody hell, Bertie, what are you doing here?' asked Jeff. He was very surprised as he knew the man well, and his two helpers, Skirty and Shirty. The two helpers were mixed-race, half white man and half Aborigine. There had been a lot of that going on in the past years, until the men were able to buy a wife of their own from England. The Aborigine women never gave in willingly, but were raped.

'We caught them red-handed robbing our mine. We also found gold they stole from us last month hidden in their mine,' said Bob.

'Are you making the charges?'

'Yes, I am,' said Bob.

'Right! You three, into these cells,' said Jeff.

'How long we gonna be here for?' asked Bertie.

'Till the circuit judge comes next week and he decides. Now, I want no trouble; stay put and shut up.'

Bob filled in the charge sheets, and Jim made his mark as a seconder, as he couldn't sign his name.

The jailhouse was very small, with space for only four prisoners, but it was all the little shanty town needed. The cells had piss-pots in them, and a bed, mattress, pillow and one blanket; nothing else, no washbasins. On the wall in the office was a rifle rack with four guns in it, all under lock and key. The only other furniture was a table and one chair, and there was a coat rack; a battered brass oil lamp was on the table unlit.

Having seen their prisoners safely interned, Bob and Jim went back to the mine. Sam was still there, but asleep. The old man just couldn't keep awake like he used to.

'Wake up, Sam, we're back,' called Jim.

'Oh, good. Everything all right?'

'Yes. I booked the charges.'

'Right, as soon as the bank is opened I think we should deposit the gold, and we bank any gold we find. We don't leave seams un-dug. We keep digging until we have all the gold we can see. Don't you agree?' asked Sam. The two boys acknowledged the idea. 'Right, it's two hours till sun-up. You boys catch up on some sleep.'

'No, I'm not tired. I will guard the gold,' said Bob.

Sam looked at him and realised his good intention to stay awake wasn't going to happen. He let Bob keep guard.

It took the best part of the morning moving the gold to the bank. It was very heavy. The gold was put into the huge safe, and they were given a receipt for it.

'When you are ready to move out of the area we will move the gold for you,' said the manager.

'I expect it will be next year on the *Great Britain*,' said Jim.

Bob looked at him. He hadn't suggested they go home in 1872. This was news to him. He would discuss this at more length with his brother. After all, he had found a girl who he was in love with, and once he had proposed he would have to consider what she wanted, though she did say she would love to visit England.

The boys returned to their mine and started by looking for the seam of gold that Bertie had said was running from his mine over to theirs. Bertie's mine was still open to visitors, so the boys looked carefully there for the tail end of the seam. Eventually they found it and tried to assess where it would enter their mine, if indeed it ever would. Having worked out where the gold should be, they attacked the area rigorously. Sure enough, after two hours of constant chipping away they uncovered the seam of gold. They spent the next ten hours digging it out. It was pure gold. They very wisely banked it at the first opportunity.

'We have a lot of gold now, Bob, more than we need. I don't want to be greedy. I feel I have enough for what I want to do in life,' said Jim.

'I feel the same way,' said Bob. 'I want to spend more time with Emilee and plan a future together.' Emilee had declared her love for Bob, though he had yet to ask for her hand in marriage.

One night, after Bob had returned from his evening with Emilee, Jim came into the hotel.

'Bob, I am in love with a beautiful woman I met in the bar.'

Bob was amused by his brother's sudden spurts of love. They happened all the time. This was the latest one. 'Tell me about her, Jim. What's her name?'

'Francisco. But she is known as Francis.'

'Where does she come from?'

'I forget the country. She said it had two names and was close by.'

'Was it New Zealand?'

'Yes, Bob, that's it, New Zealand. She really is pretty and she's three years younger than me. She is a great dancer.'

'Where does she work?'

'In the bar, dancing. Oh, boy, I think she is beautiful,' he said, collapsing into a chair.

'I expect you told her all about the gold we have found,' said Bob, feeling very concerned about what his loose-tongued brother might say to a stranger.

'No, I didn't, Bob. She asked me what job I did and I told her you and I were gold miners, that's all.'

'And you promise me you said nothing about the gold we found.'

'No! Bob, honest, I said nothing. I'm going to bed to dream of her,' he said, as he headed for the stairs. True to her promise the hotelier had given Sam and the two boys single rooms, especially as they were regular customers and she had grown to know them and like them.

Bob told Emilee and her family all about the gold theft and how he had put the perpetrators in prison.

'That reminds me, Emilee, the circuit judge calls here tomorrow to try any cases we have. I will have to attend along with my brother and Sam. Where do they hold the trials?'

'In the bar,' said Sidney. 'Been a long time since we had anyone on trial; nearly a year, I think. I expect all the townsfolk will be there; they all like a trial, especially if it results in a hanging.'

'Do you think they could get hanged?'

'Could be. Depends on the day and the severity of the case.'

'It's a pity because we all liked Bertie,' said Emilee.

'All those that knew him liked him. We'll just have to wait and see,' said Sidney. 'By the way, have you two decided when you are getting married?'

Emilee went crimson; she hadn't expected that from her father.

'Well, there's no point in hanging on. You have loads of money from the gold fields, so come on. Put us out of our misery and name the day. You do love each other, don't you?'

'Yes, of course we do,' said Emilee, looking at Bob to help her out.

'I haven't asked her yet,' said Bob, gazing at her and wishing he could place his arm round her and kiss her, yet feeling very embarrassed in front of her parents.

'What you waiting for, son? Ask her now,' said Sidney, getting out of his chair.

Her mother Grace had a smile of excitement, and great expectation, as Bob prepared to ask Emilee to marry him.

Bob gave a little cough.

'Emilee, I love you; will you marry me?' he asked her, bending down on one knee, as he had been told that was what he should do. He held her hand in his.

'Oh yes, Bob, darling. I feel I am ready to wed. I do love you.'

They kissed, still holding hands. Sidney and his wife applauded wildly. The men shook hands, and Sidney welcomed Bob into his family. Grace and Emilee hugged and kissed and cried in each other's arms.

'Mother, I need an engagement ring to show I am betrothed to Bob.'

'I think there're some rings in the shop. They're in a brown paper bag behind the pickled onions. Just go and have a look and choose one you like. You will have to wear it on your left hand to show the world you are promised to Bob.'

'Come with me, darling, and help me choose one,' said Emilee. The two of them left the room and went into the store. When they returned about ten minutes later, Emilee sported a diamond ring on her engagement finger.

'Now all you've got to do is name the day you are to wed,' said Sidney.

'What's the rush? We only just got engaged,' said Bob.

'She might change her mind,' said Sidney.

'I think the truth is that you want a wedding and a feast,' said Bob.

Sidney filled his pipe and lit it. 'That's not a bad idea, my son,' he said, chuckling to himself.

Bob and Emilee wandered off into the night, always going where others were also walking. One dared not take a chance. There weren't many eligible young ladies to be found in the town, and the menfolk were always on the look-out to find one; many of them hadn't the best intentions and when drunk they forgot themselves. Bob didn't want his young lady to be embarrassed if he could prevent it.

'Well, darling, what day shall we get married?' asked Bob.

'How about the middle of next month? It's my birthday on the twenty-first of October,' said Emilee.

'Fine, shall we go for that date?' asked Bob. Emilee agreed.

There were many more people coming into the town every day. Accommodation was hard to find and Sidney's store was making a lot of money selling tents, as there was nowhere else to live. The new arrivals were here to find gold, and there were some very nasty men amongst them. With them came more girls, gamblers and other conmen who were after your gold.

Bob wanted to move his wife out of this town and if necessary go to England. He and his brother had been in Australia for more than a year. Bob wasn't complaining; it had been very profitable and they had made a lot of money, all of it safe in the bank. Sam was insistent that the boys could keep what gold they had found. He said he would sell the mine when the boys had finished with it.

The sanitation in the little town couldn't cope with the extra hundreds of people. Sanitary arrangements were virtually no longer existent. Most of the men didn't care where they went to relieve themselves and, adding to this dire situation, the supply of river water had almost dried up.

The first case of cholera came a week after Bob's proposal. Two miners had gone down with it and were found dead in their tent. This terrible disease did not stop more gold prospectors coming and trying to get established in the town.

'What shall we do?' asked Sidney.

'I would be inclined to move well away until it is clear. The death rate will be colossal,' said Sam. 'I am going back to my own house tonight.'

'I want to take Emilee with me and stay at Sam's,' said Bob. 'I expect Jim will come with us as well; that is, if he is willing to leave his new girlfriend behind.'

Some of the men had set up blockades to stop any more entering the little town.

'Have you any tents left, Sidney?' asked Sam.

'About half a dozen. Take what you want. I think the wife and I have made our pile here.'

A group had collected in the saloon to discuss the situation.

'Cholera spreads like a forest fire,' said one miner.

'How can we prevent it?' asked another.

'They had it in Crimea when I was there. It had to do with the bogs and the drinking water. I know we had to wash our hands before eating and boil all the water. We lost loads of our mates out there; they were dropping like flies,' said a very old miner, whose beard was streaked with juice from the tobacco he was always chewing.

'They found another ten today. I'm not staying. I don't want to die for gold. We've got too many here; we need to get rid of half of them. In a week's time half of them will be gone, but still here,' said another old miner.

'Have you heard the circuit judge won't stop here? When he heard we had cholera in the town he just rode on by,' said the barman. 'Half my girls have left; they're scared.'

'What we gonna do about the prisoners in jail? We can't leave them there to die. I think we ought to have a meeting of the town council to decide what we do,' said the sheriff.

'Let's meet here at noon and decide. Pass the word around,' said the barman, who was also the chairman. They all agreed and went on their way.

By two that afternoon the saloon was packed. It looked as the courtroom would have looked if the circuit judge had called in as he was supposed to. Up the front was a table, with chairs. On either side were tables, one to seat the prisoner and the other to seat the defence and prosecution. Jeff Frisby, the sheriff, sat by and guarded the prisoners, preventing them from escaping. It had been decided by the town committee to have a court case and try the prisoners themselves.

The saloon keeper presided over the court case. His name was Wilfred Ashley. He was in his mid-fifties, medium height, rather on the tubby side, with a partly bald head.

He banged an empty bottle of beer on his table to act as a gavel. 'Order in court,' he shouted.

The saloon went quiet.

'This is a people's court to decide the fate of the three prisoners you see before you. Because the circuit judge ain't coming, I am acting as judge.'

A man at the judge's table called out, 'I call on Mr Bob Croxley to present the case of the prosecution.'

Bob stood up and told the court all there was to know about the three prisoners, right up to the time he had taken them to jail. The judge thanked him and he sat down.

The next man to stand was a man Bob had seen in the company of Bertie Crabtree. It looked as if he had been given the job of defence of all three men. His name was Mike Waters.

'I call on Mr Waters to speak in the defence of these three men,' said the judge.

'Your honour,' Mike said. There was laughter in the kangaroo court at the term 'your honour' being used on Wilfred Ashley. He, however, banged the table and called for order.

'I ain't got much to say, judge,' said Mike Waters. 'I have known Bertie for over three years and he always seemed a decent gentleman to me. I asked him about the gold charges, and he didn't deny it.'

Bob stood up. 'The accused was caught red-handed, your honour, and admitted the theft to all three of us witnesses.' He sat down.

'As I say, judge, he never said either way, leastways not to me, if he pinched it or not.'

'What about the other two men?' asked the judge.

'They plead not guilty also,' said Mike.

'Have you any defence for them?'

'No, judge, I ain't,' said Mike.

The judge had a chat with the two other men seated at his table. There was a lot of chatter while they were talking. Wilfred banged his bottle down once more and called for order.

'We, that is Gordon Reams and Mr Oliver Hardy, have discussed this case and we find the defendants guilty. We have decided the following punishment will be dished out right away.'

'The three of you will be sent from this town,' Wilfred said, 'never to return. You will be given a loaf of bread and a cask of water, nothing else but the clothes you stand up in. If any of you return you will be hanged by the neck till dead. Take the prisoners away, sheriff.' In view of the cholera situation in the town, and not being able to keep them in jail, it seemed to all concerned to be the fairest and most humane decision.

Bob and Jim were relieved that Bertie's trial had been fair. They realised that if the circuit judge had called, the punishment would have been a lot worse. That particular judge had very little concern for human life; perhaps it went with the job.

Sam came over to his nephews. 'Have you made your mind up when you are leaving here?' he asked.

'I'm just waiting for Emilee to say. Her parents have decided to stay here; of course they have the store to consider,' said Bob.

Fifteen people died in the night. A large pit had been dug in which they were placed, and lime was sprinkled on the dead. Toilet pits had also been dug and there was a heavy fine if anybody used any other facilities. The town was trying hard to rid itself of the disease.

Jim was still seeing his lady friend Francis, and he was very taken by her, so much so that he bought her a new dress and shoes. He had spent a night with her; apparently it had been his first time ever, and he couldn't have wished for a more experienced teacher than her.

'I'm in love with her, Bob,' he had said, a few days earlier. Bob was sympathetic but knew it was really only infatuation and that his young brother envied his engagement to Emilee and wanted the same.

Jim came over to the store where Bob had been discussing the move out of the town. 'Bob, she is not well. I fear she might have caught it.'

'I'm sorry to hear that, Jim, but you must keep away from her or you will die too,' said Bob.

'Can't I even go and sit by her side?'

'Not if you value your life, Jim. You can catch it so easily. I know you want to be with her, but I want you to come back to England with me, not die over here. We are moving out this afternoon. Emilee has agreed to come with us,' said Bob.

Early that same afternoon Sam and the two boys, together with Emilee, rode off to Sam's stone cottage. The sleeping arrangements were that Emilee had a room to herself. The boys said they would sleep in the tents they had brought with them.

Emilee had promised her parents that she wouldn't marry Bob without them being at her wedding. They were satisfied with that. 'Bye, Mother and Father, take care of yourselves. I am not far away if you want to come over,' she assured them, as she kissed them goodbye.

All of them felt very relieved at having left the goldmine township. Sam felt sure many more would die out there, as the disease was so quick and contagious. Jim was very sad he had lost Francis, but his brother knew it was for the best. She wasn't the sort of woman that Bob would want as a sister-in-law.

When they arrived at Sam's house Emilee wanted to take over. She saw that the house was clean, a meal was cooked and the beds were made. The men felt helpless and didn't know what to do to help out. Emilee was perfectly happy. Jim and Sam went and saw to their horses and fed them before stabling them for the night.

'How and when are we getting back to England?' asked Jim.

'By the next *Great Britain* sailing from Melbourne,' said Bob. 'We've got all the gold we need for the rest of our lives, and we can pay those that invested in us their money back with a fine profit.'

'Are we going on that boat again? The one with the captain who put us in prison?' asked Jim.

'I guess so, Jim. I can't see any other way.'

'I don't like him. I would like to get him on his own and give him a good bashing,' said Jim.

Just then Sam entered the room. 'Everything stinks of that huge fire; most of it is still smouldering. The house is fine, at least, but it's complete devastation around it. It's a good job I've got some hay stored in the loft for the horses.'

'Jim and I are going to go back to England after Emilee and I are married, which I hope will be in a few days' time. I will take her to England for the honeymoon.'

'You haven't asked me if that is OK,' Emilee called, coming down the stairs.

'Is it all right, my love?' called Bob.

'Yes, I reckon that's fine with me,' she replied.

Sam smiled. 'I can see who is going to wear the pants in your life,' he said. Bob conceded that it would be Emilee, most of the time.

'When is the *Great Britain* sailing, Bob?' asked Sam.

'I don't know. I expect the fire has put her back a few days. I will go in later today and find out; also if Emilee comes with me we could work out the best place and day for the wedding.'

'Yes, darling, be quick. I want to be your wife and enjoy all the benefits of marriage,' said Emilee, snuggling up to him.

'Have you decided how many children you're going to have?' asked Sam.

'We have never talked about it,' said Emilee, going crimson with embarrassment.

'Plenty of time for that. We want to enjoy life first. I think we would like to travel, perhaps America,' said Bob.

'Can I come?' asked Jim.

'Don't be silly, Jim; you will have a life of your own when we get back home, plenty of money in the bank. You will have all the ladies chasing you,' said Bob.

'Yes, I suppose you're right, Bob.'

'You can take the buggy into town, Bob,' said Sam.

'Thanks, Sam. When you're ready, my lovely,' said Bob.

She wasn't long getting ready and looked an absolute picture in her choice of clothes.

'My, you do look beautiful,' said Bob, helping her into the buggy.

'Thank you, kind sir,' she said, feeling very special.

'I think we will go to the docks first and see when she sails. We, my darling, are travelling first-class.'

'Isn't that expensive, Bob?'

'Yes. We are going to travel like the upper-class gentry.' After all, they had 25 lbs of gold, which would make them millionaires back home.

The ss *Great Britain* was at the quayside. There was a notice saying bookings could be made in a booth across the road and the ship would be sailing in ten days' time.

'Isn't she beautiful, and so big?' said Emilee, in complete admiration for her.

Having booked their cabin with a porthole, they also booked one for Jim. He had said he wanted second class, not first, and definitely not steerage.

'Come on, sweetheart, let's go and find a parson,' said Emilee.

After making enquiries they found a parson, a chapel and a hotel for the reception. Having seen to all the requirements for the voyage and the marriage, they went shopping.

'The first thing I want to buy you is a good diamond ring,' Bob said.

'Oh, no. I love the one you bought me from Father's store.'

'Are you sure you don't want a big diamond?'

'No, darling, I am satisfied with my big husband-to-be, called Bob,' she said, smiling up at him, and pulling him closer to her.

They bought lots of new clothes for each other, and had a fine lunch in the Grand Hotel.

'Shall we go home now, back to Sam's?' Bob asked.

'Yes. Sam's been very good to us; we will miss him,' said Emilee.

'I agree; he has been very generous giving us all that gold.'

It was beginning to get dark, but there was a glow on the horizon.

'Look, Bob, that's a fire. It looks like Sam's place,' said Emilee.

Bob knew there was nothing else nearby; it had to be Sam's house. Without a word Bob cracked the whip and set the little buggy bouncing over the hard mud-packed earth towards Sam's house. It was on fire.

Bob jumped from the buggy and looked around. 'Sam!' he shouted. 'Jim, where are you?'

The house being made of stone, only the wood and curtains had perished in the fire. They found Sam lying dead in the forecourt. He had been shot in the back of his head.

'I wonder who the swine are who did this,' Bob said. He raised his voice. 'Jim? Jim!'

There was no reply.

'I wonder if he is dead as well,' said Emilee.

'Let us both search around the area. It looks like only the two horses have been taken, though I bet they were looking for gold,' said Bob.

'Bob, I have found something, It was nailed to the door,' said Emilee. She came running towards him with a piece of paper. On it was scrawled:

If you want to see your brother again hand over half the gold. You would never have found it without our help. Signed, Bertie.

'What shall we do?' asked Emilee.

'At this present time, I just don't know,' said Bob.

Chapter 10

With Emilee's help Bob put Sam's body in the back of the buggy and drove it into town. He stopped at the police station, went in and told his story to the sergeant.

'You lot at the gold mine won't get much sympathy here,' the sergeant said.

'Why not?'

'Because you held an illegal law court and released three gold robbers. They should have been brought over here for us to deal with. This is the result,' he said, pointing at the ransom note.

'They will kill my brother, I'm sure of it,' said Bob.

'Don't worry, son, they won't kill your brother. It's the gold they're after. They know that if we catch them, they will hang.'

'I wonder where they could be. They can't be too far away because we need to see them if they are to get any gold,' said Bob. He felt very helpless and realised he had relied on Sam for answers.

'Don't go giving your hard-earned gold away, cobber,' said the sergeant. 'There's no need for that. Don't you worry, we will soon catch them, bloody murdering gold-robbing amateurs they are.'

'All right, Sergeant, we will leave it with you, and we will go ahead with our marriage plans.'

Having left the police station and handed over Sam's body, Bob and Emilee were at a loss for what to do next.

'We need somewhere to sleep,' said Emilee.

'That's no problem; we will stay at the Grand Hotel until we sail.'

'Oh, Bob, that would be nice,' said Emilee. 'Shall we get married next Monday? That's my birthday.'

'Yes, why not? It won't be a grand affair; we will hold a small reception here, shall we, at the hotel?'

'Yes, that would be fine,' said Emilee. She looked very anxious. 'We must send a telegram to my parents, to tell them where we are staying and about the wedding.'

'Once we're settled into the hotel we can telegraph them from there.'

They booked in. It was the bridal suite Bob had chosen. Emilee was most impressed. It was fitted out with all that they needed; the room was really luxurious. There was even a four-poster bed. Bob arranged for a single bed to be added to the room, as it was not the done thing to sleep together till their wedding day.

'You mustn't peep when I have a bath,' said Emilee, teasing him.

'As if I would. I will be the perfect husband-in-waiting.'

'Oh, how boring,' she laughed. They ran into each other's arms and kissed passionately.

'I'm trying very hard to save you till Monday, my darling,' said Bob.

'It's just as hard for me, my love,' said Emilee, very coyly.

Bob sent the telegram off to his potential parents-in-law and waited for a reply.

The police station knew where Bob was staying and said they would contact him as soon as they had some news. Days went by and they had nothing to offer.

Bob was standing outside their hotel when a man came up to him.

'It's Mr Crosley, isn't it?'

Bob took a moment to recognise the speaker. 'No! It's Croxley, actually, and you are Captain Gray of the *Great Britain*.'

'That's right. It's been a long time since we met,' said John. 'You have a brother, don't you?'

'Yes, Jim, but I am sorry to say he is being held for ransom and I know not where,' said Bob.

'My! That is a coincidence. I have just been released from a ransom demand myself.'

'Oh, how terrible for you, but you're free. Was the ransom paid?'

'No, I was released by two men who were going to use the place as shelter when the fire was ravaging the countryside. The man who locked me up was a passenger on my ship, and I'd put him in irons for knocking me down with his fist when I was trying to help him.'

'When was that?' asked Bob.

'On the journey we have just made.'

'You put me and my brother in jail as well, if you remember. That was nearly two years ago.'

'Yes, that's how I recognised you,' said John. 'Have you no wish to take your revenge for what I did to you?'

'No! I deserved it. I was drunk at the time and knocked the first officer down.'

'That's right. I see you are a changed man now, aren't you? Quite the gentleman.'

'Yes, a lot has happened since then. I am getting married on Monday and then we are going back to England.'

'We sail on the twenty-second of October,' John reminded him.

'Yes, I know. It all depends on me finding my brother. I can't leave without him.'

'You could try the house where I was held captive. It's out in the country, about five miles from here in that direction,' John said, pointing.

'Thank you, Captain. I certainly will try.'

'Good luck to you, my boy. I hope to see you and your new bride on my ship before long.'

They shook hands.

'Thank you, Captain.'

They went their separate ways.

Bob hired a horse next day and told Emilee he wanted to go for a ride and wouldn't be long. As he trotted along the road John had pointed out to him, he kept his eyes open in case he should suddenly come across the house used by John's captors. The ground was burnt black and every tree was a burnt-out hunk. It looked like hell had passed this way.

In the distance Bob saw a lone house and outbuildings. He stopped well short; he had no intention of being seen. There was a small drift of smoke from the chimney, but he couldn't see anyone. Bob stealthily crept back to his horse and galloped into town.

He knew he couldn't be sure that his brother was being held hostage in the house, but he hoped that was the place.

'Hello, Sergeant,' said Bob. It was the same man he had spoken to earlier in the week. 'I assure you I was most discreet when I followed up a tip-off from Captain John Gray, who had been held hostage himself recently. He told me of this disused house out in the country where Jim, my brother, might be held hostage.'

The sergeant listened to Bob, but was not impressed. 'Why is it you people always think you can do our job, and in doing so very often muck things up which we would have handled differently?'

'I have to find my brother quickly; the *Great Britain* sails in less than a week's time.'

'You can't hurry the solving of crime, young man,' said the sergeant. 'Leave it with me and we will investigate the house for you.'

'Thank you,' said Bob, feeling let down. He hoped he would get instant attention, and that his case was a priority.

He found Emilee in the bedroom combing her hair; she did look lovely.

'Any news from the police station?' she asked.

'No, we will just have to wait. It's nail-biting, isn't it?' said Bob.

'We have had a telegram from my parents; they have also booked into this hotel,' said Emilee, unable to hide her excitement over her forthcoming marriage.

'There won't be many at the wedding now, will there? We have lost two of us,' said Bob.

'At the end of the day, my darling, we only need you and me,' she said.

'And a vicar,' added Bob.

She laughed. 'Yes, and a vicar.'

There were two days left to the wedding and no sign of Jim or any word from the police.

'What shall we do if Jim is not here by the time we sail, my darling?' asked Emilee.

'I don't know, Emilee. I can't imagine going home without him, and not knowing whether he is dead or alive.'

Sergeant Jonny Biggs rounded up six policeman, and made sure they were armed and knew how to ride a horse.

'What's up, Sergeant?' asked Constable Bickers.

'We have a tip-off that the gang that killed Sam Barkley took away a man who they are holding as hostage for a load of gold. Well, they seem to be in the same house that Captain Gray was released from a couple of weeks ago.'

'That old farm building on Boxer Road. Yes, I know it. Fancy using that place after it has been used once. You would think they would pick somewhere further away.'

'I think they did it because it's handy, and they want a quick reply to the ransom,' said the sergeant. 'Come on, lads, look sharp, form up in pairs, we'll hit them at dusk. When we get near, I want no noise; I want to surprise them. OK, let's go.'

The policemen left their horses a hundred yards from the building, tethered up, and approached cautiously on foot. When they were within shouting distance the sergeant used a very basic loudhailer.

'Hello in the house. Release the man you are holding as a prisoner. We are armed policemen. You have five minutes to comply.'

The policemen spread out, covering every escape. They waited with rifles cocked. They gave the men ten minutes; nothing happened. Then the two workers who had been helping Bertie in the mine came out with their hands held high. Two policemen entered the door to the house as they came out. Shots were fired in the house and there was some shouting. The two Aborigines who had come out were handcuffed and led away.

'Jim,' said Bertie, inside the house, 'it looks like they have caught us and there is no sign of a gold ransom being paid. Here is my pistol. I want you to shoot me in the head. I don't want the indignity of being hanged. Shoot me in the head. Do it now.'

Jim reluctantly lifted the pistol. Bertie had been a good friend in the past, and despite the fact he had robbed them, Jim felt he was partly justified. He was only three feet from Bertie.

'Hurry, they're here.'

Jim pulled the trigger just before two big coppers entered the room.

He looked at Bertie lying dead on the floor.

'You shot him, then,' said a policeman. 'Well, that's saved the county the cost of hanging him.'

Then after a few minutes Jim was released and walked free. He was led to safety.

Jim sat on the rear end of a police horse, sharing it with another rider, and they rode steadily back to town. Jim was so excited at being free. He had really thought he would be killed, because the threats from the gunmen had been very real. Bertie wasn't kidding; he was desperate.

'Where is my brother and his bride-to-be?' Jim asked the sergeant.

'In the Royal Hotel, son. Off you go and enjoy your life.'

Jim hurried to the hotel and asked for Bob's room. Having found it, he knocked on the door.

'Room service,' he called.

Bob opened the door. The pleasure of seeing his brother standing there alive was too much for him.

'Jim! How wonderful to see you,' he said, with tears running down his cheeks.

Emilee came to the door and on seeing Jim she came up to him and hugged him. 'Oh, what a relief to have you back again safe and sound,' she said.

'Thank you, Emilee. What I have gone through I wouldn't like anyone else to be put through,' said Jim.

They brought Jim into their rooms and sat him down. He said he would like a coffee. Emilee contacted room service for coffee and sandwiches for the three of them.

'What an adventure you have had, Jim,' said Emilee.

'Yes, tell us about it,' said Bob.

'Well, Sam and I were working round his house, getting it back to the way it used to be before the fire, when suddenly three men appeared. They weren't on horses; they had left them tied up behind the house. All three of them had guns, and were masked with rags over their faces. I knew who they were by the clothes they wore.

'"We come for our share of the gold," said Bertie.

'"We haven't got any here," said Sam.

'"You're lying, Sam," said Bertie. He looked to his men. "Search the place, boys."

'They went into the house and near tore it apart looking for gold. Bertie stayed on watch while they searched. They came out the house. "We found a bag of coins," said one of them.

'"Give it here," said Bertie. He looked inside. "That's just for everyday expenses. Where are you keeping it, Sam?"

'"In the bank in case we should get robbed by thugs like you. It was you who got yourselves in this mess. If you had been decent men and mineworkers we could have worked both mines together. There was plenty to go round. But no, you had to raid us and steal from us. So I ain't showing you no help or mercy," said Sam, turning back to go into the house. Bertie aimed at his back and shot him. It was cold-blooded murder,' said Jim. 'Then they tied me up and we went to that house where the police found me.'

'We must have been just in time,' said Bob.

'Oh yes, you're right, Bob. They said that if there was no word from you they would shoot me tomorrow. They sent several notes to Sam's house telling where the gold had to be before they would let me go.'

'We never went back to the house again, so we never saw any messages.'

They were enjoying their refreshments. Jim was tucking in.

'Did they feed you well in that house, Jim?' asked Bob.

'No, some days I got nothing at all. You can see the weight I lost.'

'Don't worry, Jim; you will soon put that on once we are on board the *Great Britain* and sailing home,' said Emilee.

'Yes,' said Bob. 'This country is all right, but it ain't finished, is it? There's so much of the unknown about it. I wonder just how big Australia is. By the way, Jim, your room is next door.'

Jim looked surprised. He was never one to think before he spoke. 'Are you two sleeping together, then?'

'No, you stupid brother. That's my single bed over there,' said Bob.

'Oh yes, I see,' he answered, giving a big grin to Emilee.

'Your brother is being a good boy, Jim, and is saving himself for the wedding day.'

'I bet he finds that hard,' said Jim.

'My parents arrive tomorrow ready for the wedding on Monday.'

'Oh, it's all fixed up, then.'

'Yes, it's all fixed up, and we have booked you a double cabin on the second-class deck, which is what you want, isn't it, Jim?'

'Yes, thank you, Bob. I don't want first class; it's full of toffee-nosed individuals. I couldn't mix with them.'

'Well, we are going first-class; only the very best for us from now on, isn't it, my love?' Emilee leaned over towards Bob, and kissed him.

'Right, it's getting late. You move to your room next door, Jim,' said Bob.

'But I haven't got a key.'

'Don't act stupid, James; go down to reception and book in.'

Jim left the room. Bob shook his head.

'Emilee, I don't know what you think, but sometimes I think my brother hasn't got a brain.'

'Oh, don't say that, Bob. I think he is cute,' said Emilee.

The following day Emilee's parents arrived. When they saw the sleeping arrangements for Bob and Emilee they laughed their heads off.

'Talk about tormenting temptation; you two have exceeded all expectations. How have you managed to keep your hands off each other?'

'It's been hard, Sidney, I must admit, hard for both of us, but we are happy and in love and will enjoy the fruit of love even more for having waited.'

'That's all that matters, Bob. You can wait one more day, can't you?'

'Oh, you can bet we will.' They all laughed.

Jim came into the room, looking very sleepy.

'I couldn't sleep at all in that bed. It was far too soft,' he said, yawning.

'Did I tell you I met the captain of the ss *Great Britain* the other day?' asked Bob. 'It was he who recognised me. We had a good friendly chat and he said he was looking forward to seeing us with my new bride when the ship sails for England.'

'Oh, I hate the fellow. I could punch him on the nose quite easily. He liked you if you were rich, but if you were steerage-class, he despised you,' said Jim.

'Oh come now, Jim, that's hardly a fair assessment of the man. He had a difficult job to do. I acknowledge I was at fault when he placed me in irons. Forgive and forget, that's my motto,' said Bob.

'Hello, Jim,' said Sidney. 'Bob has been filling me in on the details of how you were held to ransom.'

'Yes, it was no joke, I can assure you,' said Jim, with another long yawn.

There was a knock on the door. It was a young man in a smart suit.

'I have a package for Miss Emilee Croxley.'

Emilee blushed, that being her married name which she would be known by tomorrow when she was married to Bob. She took the package and went into her bedroom. She opened the box and gazed at her wedding dress, which had been fitted for her by a local bridal shop. She tried it on to make sure the alterations she had requested had been carried out. She stood in front of the mirror and admired herself, then repacked the dress till tomorrow.

'Everything all right?' asked Bob, poking his nose round the door.

'Yes, darling, everything is wonderful,' she replied.

The whole family enjoyed the day together and looked forward to the big event, which started the following day even though there were only five of them attending the wedding. The men went to breakfast first, following the traditional etiquette that the groom shouldn't see the bride until they were in the chapel. Then Emilee and her mother went to breakfast.

'How are you feeling, Emilee?' asked Grace.

'Fine, Mother. I seem to have waited so long for today to come around. I suppose it's all down to the frustration of sleeping in the same room as your man and not yet being able to fulfil the obligations and benefits of marriage.'

'I understand, my dear. It won't be much longer. We will dress you for the wedding later.'

'I'm sorry that we are marrying in a rush, but we do want to catch that ship to England. I would have liked to invite all our friends and relatives, but it was impossible. As long as you and Father are here to see it, we will be happy.'

Later that morning, all five of them attended chapel.

'This is most extraordinary,' said the chaplain. 'We normally have a full church for our weddings. Are you sure there is no one else you want to invite?'

'Yes, Vicar,' said Bob. 'You can do a ceremony with this small number, can't you?'

'Yes, my boy, indeed I can. Well, if you're all here we will start.'

The whole thing was over in fifteen minutes, and they were over the road in the little hotel enjoying their wedding breakfast. Bob carried his bride into the bridal suite and they were left on their own till the next morning. They had breakfast delivered to their rooms, and didn't mix with their family till midday.

Sidney and Grace were delighted to see the happiness shown by the bridal couple.

'Hello. Did you sleep well?' asked Sidney.

'Yes, we did,' said Bob. 'But we had lots to talk about, and didn't get to sleep till two this morning.'

'If I had known that, I would have volunteered to act as secretary and take notes during the night. Strictly for the record, of course,' said Jim.

'Thank you, Jim, but your services weren't required,' said Emilee, in good fun.

'Well, I suppose we ought to go aboard our ship, ready for sailing this evening,' said Bob. 'Are you ready to go aboard, Jim?'

'Yes, I am. Have we checked our gold is safely on board?'

'Yes, I have done that, and here is the receipt for it,' replied Bob. He looked to Emilee's parents. 'What are you two going to do? Emilee and I are concerned about you both, especially with this cholera. Why don't you come to England with us?'

Sidney looked at his wife Grace. 'What do you think? We could go for a holiday.'

'Can we afford it?' asked Grace.

'Don't worry about that; we will pay the fares,' said Bob. 'What do you say? Come to England with us, or stay where you are and risk cholera?'

'All right, my son, we will come with you. I have a good friend looking after the store. I will send him a telegram explaining what we plan to do. The store will be safe with him.'

'So it is decided,' said Bob. Emilee was delighted at the thought of her mother and father coming to England with them.

They went to the booking office only to find that the first-class cabins had all been taken. This was a blow to the family.

'Wait here in the hotel; I won't be long,' said Bob, and he was gone in a flash, before anyone could question him.

Bob legged it to the *Great Britain*, which stood at the quay like a super athlete waiting for the gun to fire before starting a hundred-yard sprint. A thin coil of smoke was coming from her massive chimney, showing there was life aboard and the big ship was raring to go. Bob ran up the gangplank and was stopped by a ship's officer he did not recognise.

'Are you a passenger, sir?'

'Yes, I am.'

'Show me your ticket, please.'

'I'm sorry, but I have left it back at the hotel.'

'Sorry, sir; no ticket, you cannot come aboard,' he said, turning to a couple who had their tickets ready.

'But I have an important message for Captain John Gray,' said Bob.

'Do you know Captain Gray?'

'Yes, we know each other very well.'

'Wait here.'

He was only gone two minutes and came back with a steward. 'Take this gentleman to see the captain.'

'Yes, sir,' the steward replied. 'Follow me, sir.'

Bob knew his way about the lower decks but had never been in the first-class part of the ship.

'Here we are, sir,' the steward said, tapping on the door of the captain's cabin.

John appeared, and when he saw Bob he smiled in recognition. 'Hello, Mr Croxley. What can I do for you?'

'Captain, I was married yesterday and my in-laws want to come to England with us, but the booking office says all first-class berths are full. Can you help me out, please?'

'If you are willing to accept the bridal suite then your in-laws can have the one you booked. How does that suit you?'

'That's wonderful, Captain. Thank you very much. We will come aboard this afternoon. Who shall I pay for the bridal suite, sir?'

'Accept it as a wedding gift from the company,' he said with a smile. Bob was delighted and couldn't wait to get back to the hotel and give them the news.

'That's fantastic,' said Sidney. 'What a wonderful, generous man he must be. Don't you agree, Grace?'

'Yes, we will thank him personally when we meet him,' she replied.

'You don't know him like Bob and I do. He can be a hard man,' said Jim.

'Well, he would have to be. After all, he is the captain of a large ship and hundreds of passengers; it is a big responsibility,' said Sidney.

'You know he put us in chains for getting drunk,' said Jim.

'Yes, but we were drinking illegal liqueur, and the ship's officer did give us a warning,' added Bob.

'My, you have changed a lot over the last two years,' said Jim.

Bob ignored him. 'They are collecting our baggage in a couple of hours. We only take with us what we need on the journey.'

'Storage space is very limited, so just take hand baggage,' Emilee advised her parents. 'Don't worry, Mother, we can soon buy you a new wardrobe when we land.'

'This is all so unexpected and exciting,' said Grace. 'We have never experienced anything like this before. I am so grateful, Bob, for what you have done.'

The family boarded at 3pm and found their respective cabins.

'Isn't it tiny?' said Grace. 'Don't we get one each?'

'No, Mother, that's all the space you get,' said Emilee. 'We are just the same, though being in the bridal suite we do have a few more benefits.'

'I wonder how your brother is doing in second class,' said Sidney.

'I don't know, but it was his own wish,' said Bob.

'If you are settled in we can go up on deck and see some of the ship,' said Emilee, who had changed into a pretty summer dress, with a bonnet to match. They called on Jim, then went up to the top deck with him and looked around.

'There's a cow in that shed,' said Grace.

'Yes, that is to supply us in first class with fresh milk every day.'

'My, they think of everything, don't they?'

'Also, Mother, there are hundreds of sheep, pigs and birds for the table to make sure we have fresh meat every day.'

'It is a very big ship,' said Sidney. 'Did you say it was made out of iron?'

'That's right, and it takes up less sea space than an oak one the same size,' said Bob.

Captain Gray came up behind them. 'Hello. Are you marvelling at my wonderful ship?'

'Indeed we are, sir,' said Sidney.

'Let me introduce you to Captain John Gray, the captain of this ship,' said Bob.

John shook hands with all of them. When it came to Jim's turn, Jim turned away and ignored the hand of friendship. The captain was a little taken aback at the man's rudeness, but didn't dwell on it.

'Come on, I have a little time to spare; I will show you around.' They set off in a party let by John the captain.

Chapter 11

'Are we all set to go?' asked Henry. He had to rely so much on questioning those around him, due to the loss of his eyesight, but he knew they were leaving the farm today to board the *Great Britain* and return to England. It was a worrying time for him as he liked to run the farm the way he wanted it, but now he had to rely on others to do it.

'Yes, darling, the buggy is loaded. You sit in front with Mango.'

Mango was the new member of the workforce. He was part Aborigine, and had been brought up in a Catholic school where he had learnt English. He was a replacement for Mikano, who had been murdered. Unfortunately, he was unused to sheep, so he had to be taught the tricks of the trade. However, the reports from the other men on the farm were very good, and he was certainly earning his keep.

Wilfred had turned out to be a real trump. He was a youth, not a man, but he had brains, and worked hard. The men liked him and took orders from him because he had earned their confidence.

'You have a big responsibility, Wilfred, my son, but I know you are up to it, so I leave the farm entirely under your control,' said Henry. 'I expect we will be away at least three months.'

'That's all right, Father. You can rely on me.'

'Give me your hand, son,' Henry said. Wilfred placed his hand in his father's, who shook it to confirm their mutual trust and understanding.

There were three of them travelling to England including their unofficially adopted daughter Rose, who appeared to be suffering from consumption, for which there was no known cure in Australia. Mary was just hoping it wouldn't be the same back home.

'Just look at all the burnt grass,' said Mary, to no one in particular. 'The fire only just missed our sheep farm.'

Rose was looking round in wonder at all the grasslands that had been burnt out, leaving only black stumps of trees.

'What happens to all the animals in a fire? Do they die?' she asked.

'Not all of them,' said Henry. 'Many of them burrow underground for safety. Others outrun the fire, but many are burnt.'

'Oh, how terrible,' said Rose. 'Have we got a drink? I'm feeling very hot,' she added.

Mary wiped Rose's forehead, and hoped her illness could be cured by the specialist at home, in England.

Having eventually arrived at the quayside, Mango helped the family onto the ship. It was all very familiar to Mary, as she had only just arrived in Australia, though she dreaded the sea journey back to England. They found they had the same cabins as before, so Mary knew where everything was and how to stow her baggage, and she knew what to bring so as not to overload the small cabin space available. Henry was also familiar with the cabin layout, and knew where to find various places on board such as the dining room and toilets. Mary had got him a white stick so he could tap his way around the ship. This was the second time he had lost his sight, so he was used to people being helpful.

Mary and Henry had some doubts as to whether anyone would recognise Rose as being the girl they had smuggled off the ship six weeks ago. She certainly didn't look the same; she had filled out and was clean and smartly dressed. They often marvelled at what they had got away with.

Rose loved the big ship and was fascinated by all the animals on board, the hustle and bustle of all the passengers, and the children. She had been told by Mary that she would dine apart from the adults. When she saw what the selection of food was, even for children, she was amazed and tucked in with the others. She soon made friends and became especially friendly with a boy called Harold. He was ten, and Mary learnt later from his mother that he was going to England for an operation because he had bad blood. She had no idea what the new hospital could do about it, but they had suggested that they may have a cure. It was a shame because Harold was such a clever boy, and seemed to know something about everything.

The ship was leaving that evening at 6pm. There were so many people saying goodbye to their loved ones that the ship's officers were getting them off the boat early, otherwise it could take ages, and some, who hadn't disembarked as ordered, could find themselves as illegal passengers and have to pay their fare to the next port of call. It had happened before. Plus there were always stowaways. On the last trip from Australia ten stowaways had been found, and a little boy of ten, all alone. Apparently his father was sending him to school in England, and as the father was unable to travel himself, he got his son a first-class cabin and left him to his own devices.

Bob and Emilee were very happy with their accommodation. They had two rooms, a washbasin, and their own toilet. It was, said Bob, the only way to travel, as he lay on the full-size bed beckoning his wife over to join him. Emilee was busy hanging up their clothes, but was happy to fulfil his wishes. They were both very much in love.

Jim, on the other hand, had become very remorseful and depressed. Bob couldn't get a sensible reason from him as to why he was that way.

'What's the matter with you, Jim? Is it because we are in first class and not you? It was your idea, remember.'

'I know. I feel lonely at times. I wish I had stayed with my lady friend and we had died together.'

'That's just being bloody silly. You're not jealous of what I have, are you?'

'You mean Emilee? No, she's a lovely girl, I'm happy for you.'

'Have a few drinks, see if that cheers you up. There must be some nice people in second class.'

'Yes, there are, and I will drink with them later. I don't like the way the captain looks at me, as if he's keeping an eye on me and would put me back in irons if he had the chance.'

'Don't be silly, Jim. Our captain is not that sort of man.' Bob consoled him and told him to cheer up, then made his way to his suite.

Bob had noticed that the man who was in the room next to his was totally blind but seemed familiar with his way around, as if he had been here before. That night Bob and his family were invited to the captain's table, and sitting next to them were that same couple. Bob decided to make the first move in the conversation.

'Excuse my asking, sir, but is your lack of sight permanent?'

'Why do you ask, sir?' replied Henry.

'Because I have noticed how good you are at finding your way around, as if you are familiar with the ship and its layout.'

'The reason for that, sir, is because it is only six weeks since we were on this ship, berthed in the same cabins. I am going to England to see if the specialists can restore my eyesight.'

'Good luck to you,' he said. 'My name is Bob. I have just got married. My wife Emilee is sitting across the table from you.'

Henry smiled in that direction. 'Good evening, Emilee. My name is Henry and this is my wife Mary.'

The men shook hands; the ladies smiled in recognition. With introductions complete the two families exchanged small intimate details of where they were from and how they made their living. Henry was very intrigued to meet a successful gold miner; someone who had really made a killing in the gold fields was very rare to find.

Sidney looked at the menu and was surprised and delighted by the mouthwatering dishes being served that evening; there were so many choices.

Gradually the table chatter increased along with the other nine tables, all of which were full.

'I heard the captain say to the first officer that there were 350 passengers on board,' said Grace. 'That is a huge responsibility for any sea captain. His mind must be in turmoil with so much activity on his ship.'

'Here he comes now,' said Emilee, who had been looking out for his arrival. Once again, like his guests he was dressed formally.

'Good evening, all of you,' said John. 'I welcome you on board and hope you have a happy voyage. I know some of you have been on this ship before; please convey any tips you can to those who are new here. It is a fact that I personally find every voyage a new adventure. There is always something to learn. This work is never monotonous, but exciting and challenging. I just love it,' he said, with a smile to those at his table.

'Is it right that you have 350 passengers on board?' asked Sidney.

'We have 365 altogether and 123 crew.'

'My, that is a lot. It's like a floating hotel,' said Sidney.

'Indeed it is. So we have to carry provisions to keep you all fed and watered. In addition to that we carry enough coal for our engine to last us until we arrive back in England. That is one of my greatest concerns, that we don't run out of coal, as the engine is our only method of transport when the wind stops blowing, which it does, often without warning,' said John.

'Captain, am I mistaken in saying that I thought I saw guns on deck?' asked a young man in a red evening jacket with a black velvet collar and bow tie.

'Yes, that's right: we carry six eight-pounder guns on board in case of piracy. It is a known fact that the ss *Great Britain* carries gold to England. Today we carry seven tons of gold. I have in the past carried a lot more, which is a tempting target to any pirate, and there are many who still operate in these waters.'

'Wow! I didn't know that. I feel better now that my gold is safe,' said Bob.

'Your ship is truly unique, Captain,' said Emilee.

'I know. I do my best to make her the finest ship afloat. I like to ensure my passengers' comfort, and for them to feel confident that whatever personal items they bring on board are safe. I would advise any of you who have in your cabin luggage anything of value to hand it to the bursar, who will give you a receipt.'

The meal was now well under way, as was the ship. The sea was comparatively calm that evening; there was a slight swell. Three passengers excused themselves from the table and made a dash for the leeward side, as they were suffering from seasickness. The ship's engine had been turned off and the ship was now under full sail. The deck tilted to starboard, and anything not secured slid along until it met an immovable object. Luckily, the stewards serving food and wine were practised in their art and managed to get the food piping hot to those who sat patiently waiting.

Jim, who was travelling second-class, was satisfied when he sat down to be served; the food was hot and appetising. He gave a thought to those in steerage and remembered how crowded and noisy it was. He had a small single room with a porthole and was content, though he did wish at times he had someone to talk to. He made up for it at the dining table and chattered away to his fellow diners.

Jim was also drinking excessively. He had developed a taste for malt whisky while in Australia. There was a great deal of beer consumed out there because it became so hot, but after being introduced to the difference between the proprietary brands and single malts, he had changed his drinking habits in favour of the latter. He felt quite content with a good book and a malt whisky chaser, and could work his way through a bottle in an evening.

John left the captain's table after the main course and gave his apologies, for there was work to be done that only he as captain of the ship could attend to. There was a wind blowing up and the sails had to be set in case it turned to a gale. The captain of a ship in those days had to use his past experience of how the seas ran and of what he might expect from high winds. He also had to make sure his crew were aware that they were approaching an area where icebergs had been reported. The captain hardly ever got to bed before three in the morning, and he was still suffering from bouts of depression.

After nearly two hours the guests at the captain's table made their way back to their berths, or went on the promenade deck for an evening stroll. There wasn't a lot to do, and just like on the outward journey many spent the time lying on their beds, sleeping, or waiting for the next meal. Most of Bob's party were very seasick. There was nothing he could do for them. Gradually during the course of the journey they would get their sea legs, but it would take time.

Bob invited Sidney and Grace to see more of the ship, as the sea was very calm and it would be a good time to do so. They both agreed. Bob led the way, Grace followed him and Sidney came along last. There was so much to see. When John had taken them round when they had first arrived, he had been called away and had to terminate the tour. As Bob had made this journey before, he was a qualified guide.

'You have seen the top deck, haven't you, so we won't go back up there. This is the promenade deck, where we take our exercise. The captain likes us to walk at least two miles every day. He is a fanatical keep-fit man. Do you know he climbs the rigging three times a week?'

'No, I didn't. He must be a fit man,' said Grace.

'Indeed he is,' said Bob. 'Shall we go downstairs into steerage? Be careful; the stairs are quite steep.'

He had no sooner said that than with a cry of despair Grace missed her footing and fell the last half-dozen steps, landing on her head. She lay there moaning and in pain. A steward passed by, saw what had happened and said he would get the ship's doctor. They waited twenty minutes for the doctor to appear.

'Oh dear, she has had a bad fall. Wait! I will send for a stretcher party to take her to the sick bay.'

Sidney didn't know what to do. He was very upset and kept on talking to Grace, trying to console her. She tried to answer and all they could understand was that her head hurt. The stretcher party were soon on the scene of the accident and carried Grace off to the ops room. They told the men to wait outside while they examined her.

'Wait till Emilee hears what's happened to her mum; she will be very upset,' said Sidney. 'Oh dear, this would happen at the start of our holiday.'

'Cheer up, old chap. It may be nothing serious,' said Bob.

They sat there for an hour and eventually a young man with glasses and a moustache came out to speak to them.

'The lady has concussion due to banging her head, so she might get some headaches. She has been badly shaken and has damaged her hands. We will get the stretcher party to take her to her berth, where she can lie down and rest till she recovers.'

Sidney thanked the young man and said he would go back to her berth and wait for her.

'I think it would be best if Grace came into the bridal suite and I moved into her berth,' said Bob. 'What do you think, Sidney?'

'I don't know; I can look after her, and this is your honeymoon, after all. I suggest we leave things as they are.'

Emilee was spending the morning writing letters; there were so many people who had no idea where she was or that she was married. Bob entered their suite.

'I have some bad news for you, my darling,' said Bob, putting his arm round her.

'What? Is it... Mother?'

'Yes, she fell down some steps in steerage class.'

'Where is she now?'

'They are bringing her back to her cabin. Your father insists on looking after her, even though I suggested she come in here.'

'Oh, dear Mother. I must go and find her,' she said, hurrying from their suite.

She got to her parents' cabin just as her mother arrived from casualty with her head bandaged, and looking terribly white and in a state of shock. She didn't want any fuss and was content just to sit down.

'The doctor gave me some tablets and said I must rest,' she said. 'I don't want a lot of fuss; I will be all right.'

'It's lunch in an hour; can I have yours brought to your cabin?' asked Emilee.

'Yes, that would be fine, but I am not very hungry,' said Grace, leaning back against the pillows.

She had a little to eat, but went straight to sleep after that. She woke at ten o'clock that night complaining of a severe headache. Emilee wouldn't listen to her dad, and kept coming into their cabin to check up on her. She was sleeping soundly at midnight.

Early next morning Emilee came to see how her mother was.

'How is she, Father?' she asked, going over and looking at her.

'She had a good night; she never made a sound all night,' said Sidney.

'It's 9.30, time she was awake. Come on, Mother, wake up; it's morning.'

Not a sound or movement. Emilee felt her pulse; there wasn't one.

'I think she is dead, Father,' she whispered with tears running down her cheeks. 'I think that blow to the head gave her what they call concussion. I remember being told about that at school.'

'No, she can't be; she was talking to me before she went to sleep.' He got off his bunk and went to check his wife. There was no life; in fact she was cold.

Bob wondered how his mother-in-law was, and after a while followed his wife across to see.

'She's dead, Bob,' said Emilee, with tears rolling down her cheeks.

'Never!' said Bob. 'What went wrong? Are you sure she is dead?'

'Yes. We sent for the doctor; here he is now,' she said, resting her head on Bob's shoulder.

The ship's doctor arrived complete with his Gladstone bag.

'Would you mind all staying outside while I examine her?' he asked, placing his monocle in his right eye. They all did as he told them and shut the door. It was about five minutes later he opened the door.

'Yes, you are right. Fortunately she died in her sleep; at least she didn't suffer. One can never tell with head blows. I will arrange for her to be taken to the mortuary and you can make arrangements with the bursar as regards her funeral. Good day,' he said, and was gone in a flash.

Once Grace had been taken away, there was a strange silence in the family. Nobody knew what to say. Sidney went off on his own to smoke his pipe and reflect on all the happy days he had spent with Grace. Bob and Emilee returned to their room. There was a knock on their door. Bob opened it. It was his brother Jim.

'I have just heard the sad news. I don't know what to say, except she was a lovely lady.'

'Thank you, Jim,' said Emilee. 'We will let you know when the funeral is.'

'How will she be buried?' he asked.

'She will have a ship's burial at sea,' said Bob.

The funeral was arranged for two days' time at midday. There were an old man and two newly born babies being buried at the same time. On the day, there were hundreds of people who wanted to see the multiple funerals. The ship's captain was in attendance together with his first and second officers, all in their best dress. Those nearest and dearest stood together close to where the bodies were placed. A short prayer was said, and Mr Oliver was slid ceremonially into the water. His canvas-wrapped and weighted body disappeared as soon as it hit the water. Next were the two babies, whose mothers were sobbing away, and last came Grace. A short prayer was said for her. Emilee had found a paper rose, and she stuck it in the canvas stitching. Grace silently departed. The captain said a few words and the padre said a final prayer before they all dispersed.

After the funeral, refreshments were laid on as a wake for those who had died. This was one of the rare occasions when the messing arrangements permitted the mixing of the different classes of customer. 'Everyone is equal at the time of death' was John's philosophy when questioned about it, usually by some snobbish first-class passenger.

The sadness at losing Grace did take some time on her family. Everyone felt the loss and how strange it was not to have her in one's company; she was a lovely lady.

One of the worst problems on board was boredom. Every day was the same, so it was up to individuals to invent games, quizzes and competitions for everyone to partake in. The classes were still segregated, but each was asked to form an entertainment committee to run things. Nobody wanted to volunteer. They were willing to take part, but not to organise these pastimes.

In the first-class section they were more inventive and a choral society was formed which entertained the first-class passengers. There were regular church services and Holy Communion.

John Gray was usually seen talking to the passengers, asking whether everything was all right and whether there was anything he could improve on. He often challenged people to partake in various games, like whist and bridge, usually for 3d a point, which was a lot of money if one was at the losing end.

A great deal of food was wasted because of seasick passengers unable to face food. The sanitary conditions were not good and inevitably there was an outbreak of food poisoning on board. One can imagine how the passengers felt, suffering with seasickness and food poisoning together. It was terrible down in steerage class, which was where it had most likely started. There were a few deaths, mostly among the elderly and children. The ship's doctor said it was cholera. This made matters worse because all the passengers suspected each other of carrying it. The one person who had sound knowledge of the difference was Mary Harper.

Mary had been a nurse in Crimea, where there was real cholera and men were dying in their hundreds. She realised this was not the same. She spoke to the ship's doctor, who insisted the ship put into the nearest port and dump those who were ill.

Having been told to mind her own business by the doctor, Mary went to find the ship's captain. John knew Mary and Henry, having spent some time at their house during the big fire; because of this familiarity they both used each other's first names.

'Hello, Mary, how can I help you?' he asked.

'John, I am concerned about this terrible outbreak of food poisoning.'

'The doctor assured me it was cholera,' said John.

'If it was we would have hundreds dead; no, it's food poisoning, and I do know the difference.'

'What do you suggest?'

'Make sure they all wash their hands before eating and after going to the toilet. Keep the kitchen food covered and the tables in there scrubbed.'

'Do you think that will stop it?'

'I am sure it will. Not overnight, but it won't get worse.'

'Thank you, Mary. I will see your ideas are implemented right away.'

Sure enough, through strict discipline throughout the ship the illness was soon cleared up. John was very thankful for her help and said he would see she got recognition from the ship's directors when they arrived in Liverpool.

It was a week later that Mary thought she hadn't seen the captain for a few days, and she was curious as to what might have happened to him. She enquired of the senior steward, 'Where is the captain? We have not seen him about, which is unusual.'

'Yes, madam, you won't see him around for some time. He is lying sick in his quarters.'

'Can I see him?'

'No, madam, he does not want to see anyone.'

'What's wrong with him?'

'He is suffering from depression, headaches and tummy trouble.'

'Has the doctor been to see him?'

'Yes, he has done his best, but the captain isn't improving.'

'I am a senior nursing sister and have taught medicine to nursing staff in London. I have a concoction which I think will help the captain. It was developed by the nursing staff when I was in Crimea. Let me at least see if I can make him better.'

'I am sorry, madam, but it would be more than my life's worth to let anyone with quack medicines attend to our captain.'

'You do realise it was me who persuaded the captain that the doctor's diagnosis was wrong during that cholera scare.'

'I don't know what you mean, madam.'

'The doctor wanted the flags to be flown from the mast to say this was a diseased ship, and to unload half our passengers at the nearest port. It was me who advised the captain that the doctor was wrong, and what was wrong with the passengers was food poisoning, which is unpleasant, I know, but compared to cholera it is nothing. The captain passed this information on, and within a week the ship was clean again. So why not let me try? I won't kill him, and I am certain I can make him a lot better.'

The officer thought for a moment.

'You don't want him to die, do you?' asked Mary.

'Of course not.'

'He is a personal friend of ours and stayed at our house after he was kidnapped.'

'You know about that?'

'Yes.'

The officer was still very hesitant. 'All right, you may go and see him, but don't stay long.'

Mary went to his cabin door and knocked gently; there was no reply. She tried again.

'What is it?' called John.

'It's me, Mary. Can I come in?'

'I don't want to see anyone. I feel I am at death's door,' he groaned.

'I have some medication which I am sure will make you feel better. Can I come in?'

'Yes, all right, anything to improve my condition.'

Mary went into the cabin. There was no air; it was very stuffy. She opened the porthole. 'That's better; let's get some fresh air in here.'

John blinked at the daylight and managed to sit up.

'John, what I have here is made from the bark of the willow tree. It is not some quack medication. It has been tried and tested many times and is going to be commercially patented under the name of aspirin. I expect it will be in tablet form.'

She poured a dose into a large dessert spoon. 'Open up,' she demanded.

He opened his mouth in obedience.

'Now swallow.'

'Ugh, it tastes horrid.'

'It will help to cure you. When did you last eat?'

'Yesterday. I don't feel like eating. I have a very severe headache.'

'I am hoping that what you have taken will help to cure that,' she said. 'Will you eat some eggs if I have them sent up?'

'I will try,' he said.

She plumped up his pillows and made him comfortable. 'I will come back in four hours, if I may?'

'Of course you may.'

She kissed him on the forehead and left the cabin. Four hours later she returned. John was up and dressed.

'John! What has happened? Are you all right?'

'I ate those eggs you sent over and went back to sleep and now feel a different man. The medicine you gave me hasn't cured everything, but has made it a lot better. My headache has gone,' he said with a smile.

'Well, that is good. I would suggest you have one more dose of aspirin.'

'Must I?' he asked.

She nodded. 'Take it easy, John, you're not cured yet.'

'I want my passengers to see me. That way I can reassure them I am well.'

Mary knew what a stubborn man he was and left him to it, after giving him another dose of her wonder medication.

Chapter 12

The ship was now at the southernmost tip of South America. It was a dangerous area as there were many icebergs floating around. This meant that the crew had to be even more observant, because bumping into one could be the end of everything and everyone on board. They were nearly half-way home, but still had a long way to go.

John Gray was happy to be back on his feet again. He went and saw Mary, and thanked her for taking over his medication. He said he had found that although it tasted horrible it was the finest medicine he had ever taken to cure his complaints, and he felt very much better.

'Do you sometimes suffer from bouts of depression, John?' she asked him.

'Yes, I do. Why? Have you got a cure for that as well?' he said, with a smile.

'If you could tell me what is worrying you, I might be able to ease your anxiety.'

'All right! The next time I feel depressed I will call on you; will that be all right?'

Mary agreed. She was so pleased to see the change in him. He was a very good man.

The passengers on board the *Great Britain* were enjoying their voyage to England. Most of them by now had overcome seasickness and found their sea legs. The weather was sunny and there was a good wind blowing. These conditions were welcomed by the passengers.

Jim was drinking too much. It was mainly down to loneliness and boredom. He had no shortage of drinking friends, but this was his only interest.

There was one man in particular with whom he was very friendly. His name was Jake Spears. Jake had travelled out to Australia two years after Jim. He had found it unfriendly, and didn't like it.

'Why are you returning home so quickly?' asked Jim, staring into his fifth pint of beer. It seemed the knack when drinking in the ship's bar was to drink all you wanted to, but not to appear intoxicated.

'I don't like the place and I can't stand the Aussies,' said Jake, looking at him bleary-eyed.

'That's a big waste of money, ain't it?'

'No, I worked my passage going out and am doing the same coming home.'

'You don't seem to be doing much work,' said Jim.

'No, I know. I just walk around with a pitchfork and bucket in my hands and nobody questions me.' He smiled.

'Crafty blighter,' said Jim.

'What about you, Jim? What are you doing on your own?'

'I got a brother, he's just got married and they are on this ship. They are travelling first-class. I didn't want to be one of that snobby lot, so I came second-class.'

'What were you doing in Australia, Jim?'

'Digging for gold.'

'Did you find any?'

'Yeah, loads of it.'

'Where is it now?'

'It's in the lock-up in the hold.'

'Can you get to it?'

'Not without my brother being there. Why?'

'Well, you told me the other day how you disliked the captain; in fact you said you would like him dead.'

'That's true, I hate him. Did I tell you he put me and my brother in irons when we came out here and fed us on bread and water?'

'He did the same to me,' said Jake. 'And I didn't do anything. It was my mate who knocked him to the floor. It was him who had the bright idea to capture him and hold him to ransom.'

'Were you part of that ransom deal?' asked Jim.

'Yes, I was. I set everything up. I had contacts who knew the area and were only too happy to oblige with the kidnap, as long as the money was good. We were broke after that, and that is why we had to hold the captain to ransom.'

'Yes, I know all about your imprisonment. So you've got a good reason as well,' said Jim.

'Yes, of course I have.'

'What are you thinking of, then, Jake?'

'Pushing him overboard,' said Jake.

'Too risky. You might be caught and get hung for murder.'

'I'm willing to take that chance if you pay me a hundred guineas.'

'All my money is tied up in gold, and my brother has to be with me before I can get it,' said Jim.

'Tell your brother you owe it to me as a gambling debt.'

'Yes, that is a possibility, and would you be willing to actually push him over the side?'

'For that much money, yes. How about it? Is it a deal?'

'When would you do it?'

'Payment first,' said Jake.

'Half now and half when it's done,' said Jim.

'It's a deal,' said Jake, holding out his hand for Jim to shake it.

Unfortunately, there was a problem with this arrangement. When Bob heard that Jim wanted money to pay a gambling debt, he refused to co-operate.

'You cannot touch that money until we arrive in England. It is held in bond; no one can touch it.'

Jim could do nothing but go back to see Jake and tell him.

'There is only one other way I can pay you, and that is to give you an IOU, signed, dated and witnessed. Surely that should be good enough,' said Jim.

Jake thought about it for a few moments. 'OK. I will accept that.'

They shook hands again.

'All right, when will you do it?'

'I won't tell you when I am doing it. You will know he is no longer about when you hear the distress calls from everyone on this ship. There may be something I want you to do for me. I will tell you nearer the time,' said Jake.

Two days later they met again.

'Jim, I have a job for you and it's very important.'

They sat down together in the saloon bar.

'What is it?' asked Jim.

'Remember I told you I may have a job you could do for me? Well, it's this. I am going to do the job tomorrow night. I have been watching the captain, and being the sort of man he is he goes by a strict routine, with timing like clockwork.' He paused for a moment, looked around to make sure no one was listening, and took another sip of his beer.

'There is a steward on board; his name is John Prout. I have been watching what he does at night, and one of his duties is to make sure all windows are shut in the upper and lower saloon lounges. These are big windows, big enough for a man to fall through.'

'OK! But where do I come in on this?' asked Jim.

'I have managed to get a spare key to the windows in the lower saloon. I want you to go there and open a window. Make sure the light is out. Can you do that for me?'

'Why, Jake?' Jim still didn't see the significance in what he had just been told.

'Because I want to make it look as if the captain has taken his own life and jumped into the sea late at night. This will take away any suspicion that he has been murdered. It's very important you get this right, Jim.'

'All right, leave it to me. I will see it's done,' said Jim.

Jake nudged Jim's knee under the table. 'Here, take this. It is the key to open the lower saloon window. Don't let me down, Jim.'

'I won't,' he replied.

The twenty-fifth of November, 1872. The ss *Great Britain* was in the Atlantic and was on the last leg home.

Captain John Gray felt better that morning. He had slept well, and felt no pains or illness in his body. He had been ill for days prior to that morning. It was a bright sunny day, still a little cold, but it was only 6am. He carried out his morning inspection, which included pulling out anything that might be hiding dirt. Woe betide the cleaner responsible for that area of the ship found not to be up to John's expectations of cleanliness.

The ship was beginning to wake up. Children were running around laughing and having fun. John walked right through the ship. It took him over an hour, but he left no part of the ship without checking it himself.

'Blankets up to air,' he shouted out, as he walked through the very congested steerage part of the ship. 'Get your bedding up to the top deck and air it.'

One or two stopped him to ask a question, or to praise him for something to their liking. He did love his passengers, and felt a personal responsibility for their welfare and happiness. He felt so young today he considered climbing the rigging on one of the masts.

Later that day John complained of stomach pains. It was a known fact amongst the doctors and nursing staff that he did have difficulty with his bowels.

During the evening he retired to his cabin. The senior steward was told to keep an eye on him, and see he didn't want for anything. John wanted to be alone; he had letters to write to folks at home and back in Australia.

The steward called on him with a cup of tea and John was his normal cheery self. The words the steward used later, when questioned, were that when he called on him John was 'as sensible as ever'.

At midnight John proceeded to carry out his nightly inspection of the top part of the ship, the upper weather deck in particular. He would spend hours up there, often lingering till three in the morning. His personal servant passed him on his way to the upper deck. John smiled and greeted him, wishing him goodnight. John was perfectly normal as far as the servant was concerned.

John was always thinking ahead, always aware of possibilities which might affect the efficiency of his ship. He knew she was getting older and that there were now new ocean-going liners which were faster and safer, if perhaps not as clean and as well-organised.

John was certainly feeling his age. He had given a lot of thought to retiring and spending time with his wife and family. He didn't want for money, so he wouldn't need full-time employment; it seemed a sensible idea. He thought he would discuss it with his wife when he got home at Christmas. He had worked out that the *Great Britain* would arrive in Liverpool on Christmas Day. He was well aware that as a passenger ocean-going liner she was past her best years and that her numbers of passengers were gradually declining. Yes, he thought, they were both getting old and tired together.

He walked slowly along the weather deck. The bosun saw him from the bridge and had a few words with him. They were well into the Atlantic by now and had made good time from Australia. John was looking forward to getting home for Christmas. He had spent too many of them at sea.

John leaned over the rail at the stern of the ship and looked down at the frothy sea far below him. Apart from navigation lights it was very dark and quiet. He heard a noise behind him, and as he turned he became aware of a man two paces away who was charging at him. John couldn't escape the assault. He recognised his assailant as Jake Spears. There was nothing John could do. He grasped the other man's jacket tightly.

John knew what was going to happen to him; he was going to be pushed overboard. There was nothing he could do to prevent it happening. He decided in a flash that if he was going overboard, so was Mr Jake Spears. The inevitable outcome took place, and the two men went overboard together. John shouted before his body hit the water, 'Revenge my death.' Nobody could hear his plea. Perhaps he was calling to his friend the ss *Great Britain* to seek revenge for what had happened to him.

His ship was sailing away into the dark moonless night. He caught glimpses of her stern navigation lights, until she disappeared out of sight altogether. His assailant couldn't swim and soon drowned.

John trod water for a few minutes and as tears ran down his cheeks he said his farewells and prayers to his family. Eventually, as fatigue and coldness overcame him, he gave himself up to the Atlantic Ocean and slid beneath the waves. It happened in an instant. There were no witnesses.

John had a personal servant who brought him his meals to eat in his quarters. This was because John could not be relied upon to eat meals at regular times as the passengers did. These irregular meal times must have played havoc with his stomach, resulting in a lot of the bowel upset and stomach pains he complained of.

The following morning his servant brought John his morning tea as usual, only to find John's cabin and rooms were empty. He called back later; there was no sign of John. He decided to advise the chief steward.

'Mr Campbell,' said John's servant, 'there is no sign of the captain. I have been to his room twice, and the bed appears not to have been slept in.'

'Right! Thank you for telling me,' said John Campbell. 'I will alert the senior officers and arrange a search of the ship.'

It didn't take long for word to circulate around the ship that the ship's captain was missing. The crew searched everywhere. There was no trace of John, or of what had happened to him.

Jim was keen to hear what Jake had to say, but couldn't find him. He went into steerage and looked at the place where Jake slept. There was no sign of him, or that he had been to bed at all. Jim didn't say anything to anyone; he didn't want to be implicated in the captain's disappearance, though it appeared obvious to Jim that Jake had played his part in the deal.

Rumours quickly began to circulate around the passengers and crew. They ranged from suicide to murder; many didn't know how close they were to the truth.

Nobody missed Jake. He had been travelling alone, and anyone who saw his bed was unslept-in didn't give it more than a cursory glance and perhaps a light-hearted comment. The mysterious disappearance of John Gray superseded everything else on board. The fact that another man had not slept in his bed seemed of no consequence, and nobody bothered to report that Jake was missing. He wasn't officially listed as absent from steerage, and nobody came to do a head count.

Jim was relieved that he didn't need to worry any more about the IOU he owed Jake. He was very happy and satisfied that the captain was no more.

There was great concern about the welfare and disappearance of the ship's captain from the senior officers and many members of first class. They held prayers for him, and the senior officer Mr Charles Chapman, who had taken over the duties of ship's captain, said some very pleasant words about John, as a seaman and a friend. The service broke up after the hymn 'For Those in Peril on the Sea'.

Bob, Emilee and Sidney were most alarmed and distressed at the disappearance of Captain Gray. They had grown to like and respect him. They couldn't believe it.

Bob met his brother at breakfast the next day.

'I hear the captain's gone missing,' said Jim.

'Yes, and we were wondering if he had been murdered,' said Bob.

'No, I reckon he jumped over the side. Took the easy way out,' said Jim, in a light-hearted manner.

'You weren't involved with his disappearance, were you, Jim?'

'Of course not. You don't think I was that keen to see him dead.'

'Only I knew you didn't like him.'

'No. He's gone, and the ship will be that much better for it,' said Jim, walking away from the conversation.

There was nothing different in the weather until they approached Southern Ireland. This was the first land they had sighted since leaving

Australia. It brought a strange happiness and relief that they were nearly home. They did encounter some nasty fog from Ireland to England. Captain Gray would have been very happy as his ship had done the journey in sixty-five days, and he would have been home in time for Christmas.

Passengers were pouring off the ship onto the quay at Liverpool, where many had relatives waiting to take them home. There was a general air of happiness among them all. The first officer stood on the bridge and waved to them, and they responded, happy and grateful to be home.

Henry, Mary and Rose were all glad to get off the ship, and although it took two long weary days they eventually got back to London. Henry's mother Betsy had a carriage waiting for them at the station and took them to her house in Mayfair.

'It only seems like yesterday you were here,' she said, smiling and hugging the family.

'In fact it's been six months since we left,' said Henry. 'Mother, this is our new daughter Rose. Remember, I sent you a letter telling you how she came to be part of the family.'

'Yes, dear, I do. Hello, Rose; welcome to the family. I understand you are not well.'

'No, Mother, but we are taking her to a London hospital where we hope they have a cure.'

The day arrived when Mary accompanied Henry to Harley Street for his appointment. The receptionist asked her to leave Henry in the room with his case containing overnight clothes. Mary kissed him goodbye.

'I'll be back to see you tomorrow, darling. Please don't be upset if the operation is not a success. There are no guarantees, I'm afraid.'

'I know, but if he can do anything to bring me out of this darkness it would be wonderful.'

Once Mary had left, Henry didn't have to wait long for the professor to appear.

'As I said before, Henry, there is no magic cure. The sight can be lost from damage to the nervous system in the head, and as you know from your previous experience, it can be just as quickly restored. Come through to my surgery and I will have a look at your eyes.'

The professor looked into his eyes but passed no comment. 'I am going to put you to sleep before I apply my treatment. Don't be alarmed. The worst after-effect you will suffer will be a slight headache.'

He asked Henry to strip off his top clothes and slip into a surgical shirt. Then he laid him down and administered chloroform until Henry was asleep.

'Miss Clancy,' the professor said to his assistant, 'I want you to help me sit the patient up and ensure his head is level.'

Together they sat Henry up and Miss Clancy steadied him.

'Now, I want you to hold this thick pad over his forehead and I am going to give it a sharp blow, which I hope will replicate his falling off a horse and will restore his sight. I am not sure it will work, but it was a blow like that which caused the loss of vision.'

He went to a cupboard and took out a large mallet with a big, heavy head.

'Here we go,' he said, and he gave a hefty blow to the pad his assistant was holding, which, when he made contact, pushed Henry's head well back.

'Well, that is all we can do. Let him sleep off the chloroform and hopefully his sight will be returned to him.'

His assistant looked at him, amazed.

'What are you staring at, woman? There is no other cure for loss of eyesight. Now help me get him to bed in the small room.'

Mary wanted desperately to see Henry the next day, but knew she had to be patient to let the specialist do his work, so she didn't call on him till early afternoon.

When she was admitted, it was to see Henry sitting up in bed with a smile on his face which told her that the operation had been successful.

'Hello, my darling Mary. This clever man has restored my sight, and I haven't a scar or serious pain to show for it; just a small headache. It truly is remarkable.'

The professor came into the room. 'Yes, the operation I performed was a success. But you must be careful not to take another blow on your head, because the next time you might lose more than your sight. You might lose your life.'

'Thank you, doctor,' said Mary. 'We will take care. Can I take him home now?'

'Of course. My receptionist will give you my bill.'

Mary helped Henry to dress, settled the bill and returned to Betsy's house, where there was a welcoming committee waiting.

'I wonder what he did to return your sight,' Betsy said.

'I expect they hit Father on the head with a big hammer,' suggested Rose. They all rocked with laughter at the little girl's humour. Rose was placed under the care of the best specialist available. He put her on the latest drugs and said she must go to a sea side where she would get plenty of fresh sea air. This should take about three months before she was cured. He said the illness was brought about when she was in prison with her father. It was decided Henry would return to England and Mary would stay with Rose in England until she was cured.

As the *Great Britain* sat in port at Liverpool, the first officer saw Mrs Gray and one of her daughters waiting patiently on the quayside for Captain Gray to appear. It was Christmas Day, and he had promised to be home in time for Christmas.

'Hello, Mrs Gray. My name is Charles Chapman.'

'Where's my husband? Where's John?' she demanded.

'I am sorry to have to tell you that your husband Captain John Gray disappeared at sea on the twenty-fifth of November.'

'How? What happened? Did he drown?'

'I am so sorry. He didn't leave a letter of explanation. We don't know how or why he disappeared. The choices are obvious. It was either suicide—'

'That's not like John. I knew him. He would never have done that. Even if he did, he would have left a letter of explanation.'

'It could have been an accident, though unlikely, or murder.'

'Murder?'

'This is possible because John's temperament did upset some people, and someone might have seen an opportunity for revenge. I don't suppose we will ever know the truth.'

Tears were falling down her cheeks.

'Goodbye, Mrs Gray. Please call on us if we can ever help you.' He touched his cap and returned to the bridge.

The last people to leave were those who had gold in the hold of the ship; it had to be signed for and was very heavy. The ship's crew would offer the service of delivering it to the quay, where the responsibility then became the owner's, though the crew were usually given a handsome tip for their services. There was an armoured vehicle from the bank to take care of the gold. It had four men with rifles guarding it.

Jim felt elated as he was about to take his first step down the gangplank onto English soil once more. He had successfully got rid of Captain Gray. He had also got rid of his accomplice at the same time, and he had saved himself a hundred guineas in an IOU, which he had now destroyed. Plus he was back home with an abundant amount of gold bullion, which would let him live in style for the rest of his life.

He didn't notice the banana skin on the first step. And, having trodden on it, his legs shot up in the air and he crashed down on his back on the iron steps. Pain shot down the length of his body. His next sensation was of falling and banging himself all over as he careered down the long flight of metal steps to the quay. There was no one else on the gangplank to stop his fall. Eventually he came to a halt. He couldn't feel his legs. He was racked with pain and bleeding from the mouth. That was the last moment he consciously remembered, because he fell into a coma.

The remainder of his party had tried to alert him, but it was too late. They made haste to get down to Jim, who by now had quite a crowd of interested bystanders who had witnessed the horrible accident. Emilee removed the banana skin that had caused Jim to fall, and followed Jim down the steps, taking care with each one. The other members of the family followed, with Bob bringing up the rear.

There was a trickle of blood coming from Jim's mouth. One could hear the ringing of bells in the distance as a horse-drawn ambulance galloped towards the quayside where Jim lay injured. A doctor came over from the ambulance and quickly ascertained that Jim was in no condition for an examination on the quayside. The best plan was to get him to hospital. The doctor signalled to the two stretcher-bearers to load him on the stretcher.

'Where are you taking him?' Bob asked.

'To Liverpool General Hospital,' the doctor answered.

'Can you tell me what's wrong with my brother?'

'I can't be certain, but it looks like he has broken his back, and has internal injuries. It's very bad. I have given him some morphine to deaden the pain.' The next moment, with bells ringing once more, the ambulance was gone.

'Well, that's a fine homecoming for my brother, isn't it? Shall we get a cab to take us to a hotel?' They all agreed, and within minutes they were on their way by cab to the best hotel Liverpool could offer.

That evening Bob and Emilee visited Jim. The doctor came up to them before they got to his bedside.

'I'm sorry, he is in great pain, and he is unconscious. We suspect he has broken his back. If that is the case there is nothing we can do.'

'Not even if we paid for the finest doctor in the world?'

'No. They haven't the know-how to repair this injury. The chances are the spinal cord has snapped.'

'Which will mean he will never walk again,' suggested Bob.

'That's right, sir. It would be better for all concerned if he passed silently away. The pain he will be in cannot be quantified,' said the doctor.

This was terrible news for the family. Jim must have landed very awkwardly at the bottom of the gangplank.

'What shall we do now?' asked Emilee.

'I suggest we stay here a week and see what recovery he makes, if any. Depending on the results we will go about our business,' said Bob.

Jim was in a coma, but his brain was still functioning, and he could think. He thought about past events leading up to the death of his friend who had pushed the captain overboard, and somehow had fallen overboard himself. He knew or sensed that his condition was such that he wouldn't live long. He had only got what he deserved.

'Sorry, God,' he said, in his subconscious mind.

Nobody ever found out the reason for Captain John Gray's death.

However, the ss *Great Britain*, or the Greyhound of the Seas, as John Gray had lovingly referred to his ship, had revenged the murder of her captain and friend, Captain John Gray.

The End